KAT CANTRELL

THE CEO'S LITTLE SURPRISE

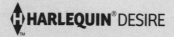

Recycling programs
for this product may
not exist in your area

ISBN-13: 978-0-373-73459-7

The CEO's Little Surprise

Copyright © 2016 by Kat Cantrell

Printed in U.S.A.

Dear Reader,

The Love and Lipstick quartet sprang out of a secret dream—I've always wanted to run a company with a few girlfriends. Owning your own business is hard work, and who better to share that with than friends? I've spent my share of time at the cosmetics counter in my favorite department store sampling lipstick and mascara. It seemed natural to combine these elements into a series of stories about four friends who fall in love against the backdrop of a threat to the cosmetics company they created. Of course, it's never as simple as that! These friends deal with secrets, lies, corporate espionage and sabotage—none of which they'd dreamed would mix with makeup.

The first book in the series belongs to Cass: the visionary. But she never envisioned that her college sweetheart would resurface, especially not in connection with the worst crisis of her career. Gage stole my heart the moment he came on the scene with his dog, but Cass was a much tougher nut to crack. I enjoyed watching these two go at it! I hope you do, too.

Don't miss the other three books in this series about Cass's friends and business partners.

I love to hear from readers. Find out where to connect with me online at katcantrell.com.

Kat Cantrell

The only prayer Gage had of cracking that ice was to give her something sizzling hot to grab on to with both hands.

"Your point—if I recall—was that you'd use all the information at your disposal to seduce me," Cass murmured throatily. "I don't think you have a shot."

"Guess there's only one way to find out."

The irresistible draw between them sucked him in, and finally his arms closed around her, and her mouth sought his. A scorching kiss ignited the pent-up emotions and desire Gage had been fighting since he'd first laid eyes on Cass in the parking lot of her building.

Yes. Her tongue darted out in a quest for his and he lost himself in the sensation of her hot flesh. She tasted of wine and familiarity.

Memories zipped by, of Cass spread out under him, hips rolling toward his in a sensuous rhythm, hair spread out, her gaze hot and full of anticipation and pleasure as they came together again and again. Memories of her laughing with him, challenging him, filling him.

He wanted her. Just like that. Right now.

* * *

The CEO's Little Surprise is part of the Love and Lipstick quartet: for four female executives, mixing business with pleasure leads to love!

Kat Cantrell read her first Harlequin novel in third grade and has been scribbling in notebooks since then. She writes smart, sexy books with a side of sass. She's a former Harlequin So You Think You Can Write winner and an RWA Golden Heart® Award finalist. Kat, her husband and their two boys live in north Texas.

Books by Kat Cantrell

HARLEQUIN DESIRE

Marriage with Benefits
The Things She Says
The Baby Deal
Pregnant by Morning
The Princess and the Player
Triplets Under the Tree
The SEAL's Secret Heirs

Happily Ever After, Inc.

Matched to a Billionaire
Matched to a Prince
Matched to Her Rival

Newlywed Games

From Ex to Eternity
From Fake to Forever

Love and Lipstick

The CEO's Little Surprise

Visit her Author Profile page at Harlequin.com, or katcantrell.com, for more titles.

One

By the time Gage Branson's tires hit the Dallas city limits, Arwen had started howling along with the radio. Not for the first time since leaving Austin, Gage questioned the wisdom of bringing his dog on a business trip.

Of course, it wasn't a normal business trip—unless showing up at your ex-girlfriend's office building unannounced and uninvited counted as customary. And Arwen wasn't a normal dog. She was his best buddy, and the one and only time he'd left her at one of those pet hotels, she'd refused to speak to him for a week.

Arwen shared Gage's love of the open road and honestly, he didn't mind the company as he drove to Dallas to collect a long overdue debt from the CEO of Fyra Cosmetics.

GB Skin for Men, the company he'd just pushed into the billion-dollar-a-year category, had enjoyed a good run as the top skin-care line of choice for the discerning guy who spends time in the elements: professional athletes, outdoorsmen, even the occasional lumberjack.

Gage had spent millions designing a new product to heal scars. The product's launch a month ago had outperformed his carefully executed publicity strategy. GB Skin instantly cornered the market. But now his former lover's company was poised to steal his success out from under him with a product of their own. That wasn't going to happen.

A Black Keys song blasted through the speakers and the howling grew unbearable.

"Arwen! Really. Shut up."

She cocked her ginger-colored head and eyed Gage.

"Yeah, never mind," Gage grumbled good-naturedly and flicked off the music.

The exit for Central Expressway loomed and Gage steered the Hummer north. He drove a few miles and before long, he rolled into the parking lot at the headquarters for Fyra Cosmetics.

Nice. Of course, he'd done an internet search for pictures before driving up from Austin. Just to check out the company Cassandra Claremont had built alongside her business partners–slash–friends after graduating from the University of Texas. But the internet hadn't done justice to the sharply modern, glass and steel, five-story building. Cass's multimillion-dollar cosmetics company lived and breathed inside these walls, and the deep purple Fyra logo dominated the landscape.

"Stay here and keep your paws off the gearshift," he muttered to Arwen and got the trademark vizsla smile for his trouble. It was a cool day, so he parked in the shade and left her in the car with the windows cracked.

Cass had done very well for herself thanks to him. Gage *had* been her mentor for eight months and turnabout was fair play. She owed him. And he'd help her see that by reminding her of how he'd guided her at a time when she had no idea how to navigate the shark-infested waters of the cosmetics industry.

With any luck, Cass would be curious enough to see him on short notice. Gage couldn't call ahead and lose the advantage of surprise. Not when he was here to get his hands on Cass's secret formula.

So secret, he shouldn't even know about it since it wasn't on the market yet. His sources had whispered in his ear about a miracle formula developed in Fyra's labs that worked with a body's natural healing properties to eliminate wrinkles and scars. His intel adamantly insisted it was better than his. And he wanted it.

You didn't spring that kind of request on anyone over the phone, not even a former girlfriend. They hadn't even spoken in eight or nine years. Nine. Maybe it was closer to ten.

"Gage Branson. To what do I owe the pleasure?"

The husky feminine voice raked over Gage from behind before he'd managed to get ten feet from the Hummer.

He spun to face the speaker and did a double take. "Cass?"

"Last time I checked." High-end sunglasses covered her eyes, but her tone conveyed a hint of cool amusement just fine. "Did I leave my face in my other purse again?"

"No, your face is right where I left it." Gorgeous and attached to a hell of a woman.

But *this* überchic version in five-inch heels and a sexy suit with cutaway panels at her hips did not resemble the Cassandra Claremont who lived in his memories. Her voice wasn't even the same. But something about the way she held herself was very familiar. Confidence and the ever-present "look but don't you dare touch" vibe had always been a huge part of her attractiveness.

Obviously *he* hadn't changed much since graduate school if she'd recognized him from behind.

"Moving into the dog transportation business, are you?" she asked blithely.

He glanced at the Hummer. "You mean Arwen? Nah. She's just company for the drive. I came up from Austin to see you, actually. Surprise."

"Do you have an appointment?"

The lack of question in that question said she already knew the answer. And wasn't planning to adjust her calendar one tiny bit, even for an old boyfriend. He'd change that soon enough.

"I was hoping you'd see me without one." He grinned, just to keep things friendly. "You know, for old times' sake."

His grin grew genuine as he recalled those old times. Lots of late-night discussions over coffee. Lots of inventive ploys to get Cass's clothes off. Lots of hot and truly spectacular sex when she finally gave in to the inevitable.

She pursed her lips. "What could we possibly have to say to each other?"

Plenty. And maybe a whole lot more than he'd originally come to say. Now that he was here and had an eyeful of the new, grown-up Cass, a late-night dinner and a few drinks with a former lover had suddenly appeared on his schedule for the evening.

Everyone here was an adult. No reason they couldn't separate business from pleasure.

"For one, I'd like to say congratulations. Long overdue, I realize," he threw in smoothly. "I've been following along from afar and what you've accomplished is remarkable."

Once her name had been dropped in his lap as a potential game changer, he'd searched the internet for details, first with an eye toward how well she was executing his advice and eventually because he couldn't stop. Strangely, he'd liked seeing her picture, liked remembering their relationship. She was one of a small handful of women from his past that he recalled fondly, and for a guy who held on to very little in his life, that was saying something.

"Thank you." She inclined her head graciously. "It was a group effort."

He waited for her to say she'd been following his entrepreneurial trajectory in kind. Maybe a congrats or two on the major retail distribution deals he'd scored in the past few years. An attaboy for Entrepreneurs of America naming him Entrepreneur of the Year. If nothing else, Fyra's CEO should be brushing up on her competition the way he had.

Nada. She hadn't been a *little* curious about what he'd been up to? Was their time together such a blip in her life that she'd truly not cared?

But then, their affair had been brief, by design. Once he'd escaped his restrictive childhood home and overprotective parents, he'd vowed to never again let his wings be clipped. He owed it to his brother, Nicolas, to live on the edge, no regrets. To experience all the things his brother never would thanks to a drunk driver. Sticking to one woman didn't go with that philosophy and Gage liked his freedom as much—or more—than he liked women, which meant he and Cass had parted ways sooner rather than later, no harm, no foul. He could hardly blame her for not looking back.

"Come on." He waved off her "group effort" comment. "You're the CEO. We both know that means you call the shots."

She crossed her arms over that sexy suit, drawing attention to her breasts. In spite of the cool breeze, the temperature inched up a few degrees.

"Yes. Because someone has to. But Trinity, Harper, Alex and I run this company together. We're all equal owners."

Yeah, he'd figured she'd say that. The four women had been inseparable in college and it wasn't hard to imagine they'd extended their tight circle into the company they'd created together. Fortunately, he'd always gotten along with the quartet of savvy females, but Cass was the one he had his sights set on. She'd make this deal happen.

"Can we take this inside?" Hoping she'd like the idea of getting behind closed doors as much as he did, he sidled closer. "I'd like to catch up."

"Gage."

Her husky voice wound through him as she moved closer in kind, tilting her head toward his in a way that shouldn't feel as intimate as it did. A hint of jasmine filtered through his senses and it was a powerful punch. "Yeah, Cass?"

"You can save the 'Kumbaya,'" she murmured. "You're here because you've heard about Fyra's breakthrough formula and you want it."

Back to business, then.

He grinned and reined in his thundering pulse. Going toe-to-toe with Cass was such a turn-on. Smart, sexy women who didn't take any crap had always floated his boat. "Am I that easy to read?"

Cass laughed in his ear, a throaty sound he instantly wanted to hear again. "I'm afraid so. Sorry you've wasted your time. The formula is not for sale."

All right, then. Cass needed persuasion to see how his

tutelage had launched her into the big leagues. He'd anticipated that.

"Of course it isn't. Not to the rest of the world. But I'm not one of the masses," he reminded her. "I'm not unreasonable. I'll pay fair market value."

He turned his head at just the right angle to almost bring their lips together. The pull between them was magnetic, and he nearly forgot for a second that he'd instigated this sensual tease to get him closer to his goal—the formula.

She didn't flinch, holding herself rock steady. "You think you have special rights because of our former relationship? Think again."

His element of surprise hadn't worked to catch her off guard and, for some reason, that made her twice as attractive. Or maybe the unexpected draw had come about because they were equals now. It was an interesting shift in their dynamic he hadn't expected, and it was throwing him off.

So he'd up his game. Gage had never met a woman he couldn't charm. When he wanted something, he got it. "That's no way to talk to an old friend."

If he moved an inch, they'd be touching. He almost did it, curious if she still felt the same—soft, exciting and warm. Except he had the distinct impression Cass was all business and little pleasure these days. And that she wasn't interested in mixing them up.

"Is that what we are?"

There came that sexy laugh again and it did a powerful number on his already-primed lower half. She really shouldn't be so intriguing, not with his agenda and the lost element of surprise. But all of that actually heightened his sense of awareness, and he had a sharp desire to get under her skin the same way she'd managed to get under his.

"Friends. Former lovers. At one time, mentor and student."

"Mmm. Yes." She cocked her head. "You've taught me a lot. So much that I'm running a successful company I need to get back to. You'll excuse my rudeness if I request you make an appointment. Like anyone else who wants to talk business."

All at once, her heat vanished as she pulled away and clacked toward the entrance to her building. Ouch. He'd been relegated to the ranks of "anyone else."

He let her go. For now.

There was no way a former pupil of his was going to take away even a single point of his market share, and he'd pay handsomely to ensure it. But one had to do these things with finesse.

Remind her of what you've done for her. Remind her how good it was.

The voice in his head was his own conscience. Probably. But sometimes he imagined it was Nicolas guiding him from beyond the veil. A big brother's advice in times of need, which usually led Gage down the path of living life to the fullest. Because Nicolas couldn't.

The philosophy had never steered Gage wrong before.

He wasn't about to stop listening to sound advice now, especially when it aligned with what he wanted. Cass clearly needed a good, solid reminder of how tight they'd been. So tight, he knew every inch of her body.

Your best strategy is to use pleasure to influence business.

Nicolas had spoken. And that pretty much solidified Gage's next steps because that genie wasn't going back in the bottle. He wanted her. And her formula. If he did it right, one would lead to the other.

He gave her a good five minutes and went after her.

Turnabout was fair play in love *and* cosmetics.

* * *

Hands shaking, Cass strode to her office and checked her strength before she slammed the door behind her. That would only invite questions and she had no answers for why her entire body still pumped with adrenaline and... other things she'd rather not examine.

Okay, that was a flat-out lie. Gage Branson was the answer, but why seeing him again so severely affected her after all of this time—*that* she couldn't explain.

God, that smile rocked her to the core, even all these years later. And his still-amazing body had been hidden underneath casual-Friday dress, when it should clearly be on display in a pinup calendar. He'd always had the messiest, most casually cut hair that somehow managed to look delicious on him. Still did. Oh, yes, he was just as sexy and charismatic as he'd always been and she hated that she noticed. Hated that he could still put a quiver in her abdomen. Especially after what he'd done.

Breathe. Gage was just a guy she used to know. Put that on repeat a thousand times and maybe she'd finally believe it. Except he wasn't just a guy from college; that was the problem.

Gage Branson had broken her.

Not just her heart, but *her*. Mind, body and soul. She'd fallen so hard for him that the splat hadn't even registered. Until he casually declared their relationship over, and did she want the clothes back that she'd left at his place?

Nine years later and she was still powerless to move on, unable to fall in love again, incapable of forgetting and far too scarred to forgive. And that's why her hands were still shaking. Pathetic.

The only positive was she felt certain Gage hadn't picked up on her consternation. God forbid *he* figure out how greatly he'd affected her. Emotions had no place here, not at work, not in her personal life. *No place.* That's the most important lesson she'd learned from her former mentor. Thankfully, he'd taken her advice to make an appointment without too much protest, giving her much-needed regroup time.

Her phone beeped, reminding her she had five minutes until the meeting she'd called would begin. Five minutes to put her thoughts together about how Fyra should handle the leak in the company. Someone reprehensible had publicized Harper's nanotechnology breakthrough before they'd even gotten FDA approval or a patent. Five minutes, when she should have had an hour, but didn't because of the car wreck on Central and the surprise appearance of the man who'd laced her nightmares for nearly a decade.

And maybe a few need-soaked dreams. But he didn't have to know about that.

Great. This was exactly what she needed, a come-to-Jesus meeting with Trinity, Harper and Alex so soon after locking horns with the offspring of Satan. Who was here strictly because of a leak that never should have happened.

Well, she'd have to get her wild swing of emotions under control. *Now.* It wasn't as though she didn't already know how she felt about the leak—sick, furious and determined to find the source. They'd not only lost a potential competitive advantage, until they figured out who had spilled, there was also no guarantee the same person wouldn't leak the secret formula—or steal it.

But five minutes was scarcely enough time to settle her racing heart before waltzing into a room with her best friends, who would see immediately that Something Had Happened. They'd probably also realize "Something" had a man's name all over it.

Working with people who'd held your hair when you drank too much and borrowed your clothes and sat with you in a tight huddle at your grandfather's funeral meant few secrets. Most of the time, Cass appreciated that. Maybe not so much today.

In the bathroom, she patted her face with a blotting cloth and fixed her makeup, which was equal parts wardrobe and armor.

No one saw through Cass when she had her face on—with the right makeup, no one had to know you were hurting. The philosophy born out of the brokenness Gage had left her with had grown into a multimillion-dollar company. Best Face Forward wasn't just the company tagline, it was Cass's personal motto.

No man would ever put a crack in her makeup again.

Fortified, Cass pasted on a cool smile and exited the bathroom. Only to run smack into Fyra's receptionist, Melinda. Her wide eyes spelled trouble as she blurted out, "There's an extremely persistent man at the front desk who seems to believe you have an appointment with him."

Gage. When she'd said make an appointment, she meant for later. Much later.

Her not-so-settled nerves began to hum. "I don't have an appointment with him. I have a meeting."

"I told him that. But he insisted that you'd scheduled time with him, and he drove all the way from Austin." Melinda lowered her voice. "He was very apologetic and sweet about it. Even asked if there was a possibility you accidentally double booked your appointments."

Did his audacity have no end?

The stars in Melinda's eyes were so bright, it was a wonder she could still see around Gage's charm. Well, Cass didn't suffer from the same affliction. "When have I ever done that?"

"Oh, I know. Never." Her shoulders ducked slightly.

"But I…well, he asked if I'd mind checking with you and he just seems so sincer—"

"Why is Gage Branson in our reception area?" Trinity Forrester, Fyra's chief marketing officer, snapped, her short, dark hair nearly bristling with outrage. Since Trinity possessed the main shoulder Cass had cried on back in college, the statement was laced with undercurrents of the "hold me back before I cut off his fingers with a dull blade" variety.

Cass stifled a sigh. Too late to have Melinda throw him out before anyone saw him. "He's here with a business proposition. I'll take care of it."

As the woman in charge, she should have taken care of it in the parking lot once she'd figured out he wanted her formula. But he'd been so… *Gage*, with his wicked smile. He fuzzled her mind and that was not okay.

This was strictly business and she would die before admitting she couldn't handle a competitor sniffing around her territory.

"That's right." Trinity crossed her arms with a smirk. "You take care of it. You toss him out on his well-toned butt. Shame such a prime specimen of a man is riddled with health problems."

Melinda's gaze bounced back and forth between her employers, clearly fascinated by the exchange. "Really? What's wrong with him?" she asked in a stage whisper.

"He's got terrible allergies to commitment and decency," Trinity explained. "And Cass is going to hand him his hat with class. Can I watch?"

Strangling over a groan, Cass shook her head. This was her battle, and there was no way she'd deal with Gage for a second time today in front of a bevy of onlookers. "It's better if I talk to him in my office. Trinity, can you tell Alex and Harper I'll be there in a few minutes?"

Trinity harrumphed but edged away as Cass stared her down. "Okay. But if you're robbing us of the show, you better come prepared to spill all the details."

With Melinda dogging her steps—because the receptionist likely didn't want to miss a thing at this point—Cass marched to the reception area.

Arms crossed and one hip leaning on the desk as if he owned it, Gage glanced toward her as she entered, his deep hazel eyes lighting up at the sight of her. His slow smile set off a tap dance in her abdomen. Which was not okay. It was even *less* okay than his ability to fuzzle her mind.

Steeling her spine against the onslaught of Gage's larger-than-life personality, she jerked her head toward the hallway. "Five minutes, Mr. Branson. I'm late for a board meeting."

"Mr. Branson. I like the sound of that," he mused, winking. "Respect where respect is due."

Flirting came so naturally to him, she wondered if he even realized when he was doing it. She rolled her eyes and turned her back on his smug face, taking off toward her office in hopes he'd get lost.

He drew abreast with little effort, glancing down at her because he still topped her by several inches no matter how high her heels were, dang it. His powerful masculinity dominated the small hallway that had always seemed quite large enough for every other person who'd accompanied her to her office.

"Trying to score the first one-minute mile? You can't outrun me barefoot, let alone while wearing icepick stilettos." He eyed them appreciatively, his too-long hair flopping over his forehead. "Which I like, by the way."

Her toes automatically curled inside her shoes as heat swept over her skin. "I didn't wear them for you."

Why had she thought taking care of this in her office

was a good idea? She should have gone to her board meeting and had Melinda tell Gage to take a hike.

But he would have just shown up over and over again until she agreed to an appointment.

So she'd get rid of him once and for all.

Two

When she halted by her open office door, Gage raised a brow as he read its deep purple placard. "Chief enhancement officer?"

His amused tone rankled but she just smiled and silently dared him to do his worst. "Branding. We put incredibly careful thought into every single aspect of this business. Seems like I had a mentor once who taught me a few things about that."

He grinned in return and didn't acknowledge her sarcasm. Nor did he say a word about her outstretched arm, choosing to humor her and enter first as she'd meant him to, but he didn't miss the opportunity to brush her, oh, so casually. She pretended the skin he'd just touched wasn't tingling.

"Yeah, we did have a few lively discussions about business strategies," he mused. "Branding is why I drive a green Hummer, by the way."

Cass had decorated her office with the same trademark Fyra deep purple hue, down to the glass-topped desk and expensive woven carpet under it. He took it all in with slightly widened eyes.

"Because you want everyone to see it and think GB Skin has zero environmental consciousness and its owner is obnoxious?" she asked sweetly before he could make a crack about her decor.

Sleek and modern, the offices had been decorated by an expensive, trendy uptown firm. It had cost a pretty penny, but the results had been worth it. This company was hers, from the baseboards to the ceiling and she loved it. They'd moved to this building three years ago, once Fyra posted its first annual revenue of fifty million dollars. That was when she knew they were going to make it.

She'd do whatever she needed to do in order to keep her company alive.

He laughed as he slid into a purple chair and then swept her with a pointed once-over. "You know the name of my company. I was starting to think you didn't care."

How did he manage to make understanding the competitive landscape sound so...*personal*? It was a skill he'd clearly bargained with the devil to obtain.

"I'm good at what I do. Of course I know the names of my competitors." Cass remained standing near the door. Which she pointedly left open. "You've got your appointment. And about three minutes to tell me why you didn't take the no I gave you earlier and run back to Austin."

Casually, he swiveled his chair to face her and waved a hand to the empty chair next to him. "Sit and let's talk."

She didn't move. There was no way she could be in close quarters with him, not on the heels of their earlier encounter when he'd barely breathed on her and still managed to get her hot and bothered. At least by the door, she had a shot at retaining the upper hand. "No, thanks. I'm okay."

"You can't keep standing. That tactic only works if you inflict it on someone other than the person who taught it to you," he said mildly.

The fact that he saw through her only made it worse.

"Really, Gage," she snapped. "Fyra's executives are waiting in a boardroom for the CEO to arrive. Cut the crap. Why are you here?"

His expression didn't change. "The rumors about your formula are true, right?"

She crossed her arms over the squiggle in her stomach. "Depends on what you've heard."

"*Revolutionary* is the word being thrown around," he said with a shrug. "I've heard the formula works with your natural stem cells to regenerate skin, thus healing scars and eliminating wrinkles. Nanotech at its finest."

She kept her expression schooled, but only just. "I can neither confirm nor deny that."

Her lungs hitched as she fought to draw a breath without alerting Gage to her distress. The leak was worse than they'd assumed. When Trinity had stormed into Cass's office yesterday to show Cass the offending blurb in an online trade magazine, she'd read the scant few lines mentioning Fyra's yet-to-be released product with horror. But it could have been so much worse, they'd assured each other. The trade magazine had few details, especially about the nanotechnology, and they'd hoped that had been the extent of the information that had traveled beyond their walls.

Apparently not.

It was a disaster. Full-blown, made even worse by Gage's arrival on the scene.

Gage watched her carefully, his sharp gaze missing

nothing. "But if my intel is correct, a formula like that might be worth about a hundred million or so. Which I'm prepared to pay."

Oh, no, he had *not* just dropped that sum on her. She shut her eyes for a blink. Money like that was serious business, and as the CEO, she had to take his offer to the others for due consideration.

But she knew her friends. They'd agree with her that the formula was priceless. "I told you, the formula isn't for sale."

He stood suddenly and advanced on her, clearly over the power play she'd instigated by standing by the door. The closer he got, the harder her pulse pounded, but she blinked coolly as if lethally sexy men faced her down on a daily basis.

"It's smart business to consider all opportunities," he said as he leaned against the doorjamb not two feet from her. "If you sell, you don't have to worry about little things like FDA approval and production costs and false-claim lawsuits. You just roll around in your millions and leave the hard work to someone else."

The scent of clean forest and man wafted in her direction.

"I'm not afraid of hard work," she stated firmly as she fought to keep from stepping back, out of the line of his masculine fire. It was a battle of wills, and if she fled, he'd figure out how much he truly affected her.

The man was a shaman, mystical and charismatic. One glance, and she'd follow him into his world of hedonistic pleasure. Or at least that had been true in college. She'd learned a few tricks of her own since then, along with developing a shield around her fragile interior.

His gaze held her captive as he reached out and tucked

a chunk of hair behind her ear, his fingers lingering far longer than they should have.

"What *are* you afraid of?" he asked softly, his expression morphing into something almost…warm.

You. She swallowed. Where had that come from? Gage didn't scare her. What scared her was how easily she forgot to control her emotions around him.

This cat-and-mouse game had veered into dangerous territory.

"Taxes," she muttered inanely and ignored the way her pulse raced.

When was the last time she'd been touched? Months and months. She'd developed a reputation among single men in Dallas as a man-eater and unfortunately, that just made her even more popular as men vied for her attention so they could claim victory. Mostly she just shut them down because the whole scene exhausted her.

And she couldn't lose sight of the fact that the reason she chewed up men and spit them out was staring her in the face. He was very dangerous indeed if she'd forgotten for a second the destruction he'd caused.

And that's when it hit her. She was handling Gage all wrong.

This wasn't college and Gage wasn't her mentor. They were equals. And he was on her turf. That meant she called the shots.

If he wanted to play, she'd play.

Once Gage had tucked the errant lock of hair behind her ear, he'd run out of legitimate excuses to have his hands on her. Which didn't keep him from silently running through a litany of illegitimate excuses.

"Gage," she murmured throatily and the base of his spine heated. "The formula's not for sale. I have a board meeting. Seems like we're done here…unless you've got a better offer?"

Her eyelids lowered to half-mast and she didn't move, but the sensual vibe emanating from her reached out and wrapped around him, drawing him in. Those cutaway panels at her waist would fit his palms perfectly and with any luck, the mesh inserts would allow him to feel her while fully clothed. The thought sent a rush of blood through his veins and the majority of it ended up in a good, solid erection that got very uncomfortable, very fast.

"I just might have something in mind," he said, his vocal chords scraping the low end of the register. God, she'd even affected his voice.

Down boy. Remind her why the formula is *for sale… but only to you.*

Yeah, he needed to get back on track, pronto, and stop letting her get into his head. He dropped his hand but leaned into her space to see about turning those tables on her. "You're doing amazing things here, Cass. I'm proud of what you've accomplished.'

Wariness sprang into her gaze as she processed his abrupt subject change. "Thank you. I'm proud of what the girls and I have built."

He crossed his arms before an errant finger could trail down the line of her throat. Because his lower half wasn't getting the message that the goal here was to get *her* hot and flustered. Not the other way around. "Remember that project I helped you with for Dr. Beck's class?"

That was before they'd started sleeping together. He didn't recall being so magnetically attracted to Cass back then. Sure he'd wanted to get her naked. But at twenty-four, he'd generally wanted women naked. These days, his taste was a bit more refined, but no woman he'd dated over the years had gotten him this hooked, this fast.

Of course, he never looked up his old girlfriends. Maybe any former lover would affect him the same. But he couldn't imagine that would be true.

Her eyes narrowed a touch. "The project where I created a new company on paper, complete with a marketing plan and logo and all of that?"

"That's the one," he said easily. "You got an A plus, if memory serves. Except you didn't do that alone. I was right there every step of the way. Guiding you. Teaching you. Infusing you with CEO superpowers."

In fact, he'd done such a good job, here he was smack in the middle of her corporation negotiating over a Fyra product that was better than his. He appreciated the irony.

An indulgent smile bloomed on her face and he didn't mistake it for a friendly one. "Nothing wrong with your memory. As much as I'm enjoying this trip down memory lane, if you have a point, now would be the time to make it."

"Your success here…" He waved a hand at her office without taking his eyes off her. "Is amazing. Your C-suite is unparalleled. But you didn't get here without me. I'm a big factor in your success."

"Yes, you are," she agreed readily. Too readily. "You taught me some of the most important lessons I've learned thus far in my life. Fyra's business philosophy grew 100 percent out of my experience with you."

She blinked and undercurrents flowed between them but hell if he could figure out what they were. Regardless, it was a great segue. Exactly what he'd hoped for.

"I'm glad you agree. That's why I'm here. To collect on that long-outstanding debt."

"Oh, really?" Her head tilted slightly as she contemplated him. "Do tell."

"You know what I'm talking about. Without me, Fyra

might never have existed. You might never have achieved your goals, particularly not to this degree. Don't you think turnabout is fair play?"

"Hmm." She touched a finger to her cheek. "Turnabout. Like I owe you for what you've done. That's an interesting concept. It's kind of like karma, in a way."

"Kind of."

But he didn't like the comparison, not the way she said it. Karma was rarely a word used in the context of reward. More like you were getting what you deserved.

"What I'm saying," he interjected smoothly before this conversation went in a direction he didn't like. "Is that I want to buy your formula. My role in your success should be a factor in your decision-making process. In all fairness, you do owe me. But I'm fair, too. I'm not asking you to *give* me the formula for old times' sake. One hundred million dollars is a lot of tit for tat."

He watched her as she filtered through his argument, but her expression remained maddeningly blank.

"Here's the thing, Gage." She leaned in, wafting a whole lot of woman in his direction. "You did teach me and I'm grateful. But you must have been sick the day they taught corporate structure, so I'll clue you in. Again. I'm a quarter owner in Fyra. We're missing three-quarters of the decision makers, none of whom *owe* you a thing. I'll take your offer for the formula to the board and we'll consider it. Period. That's how business works."

Her mouth was set so primly, he had the insane urge to kiss her. But they were just getting into the meat of this and he needed to hone his focus. Not lose it entirely.

So he grinned instead and waved off her protest. "Not in the real world, honey. You need to get out more if that's your best line of defense. Deals are done and undone across the globe based on exactly that. Companies don't make decisions. People do and rarely are they united."

"Fyra is," she insisted. "We're a team."

"I hope that's true," he said sincerely. "If so, then it's in your best interests to convince them to sell. How would they feel about their CEO not honoring this lingering debt?"

Her brows drew together but it was the only outward sign she gave that she'd heard the underlying message. This was business at its core and he was not leaving Dallas without that formula. It had become more than just about ensuring Fyra didn't take any of his market share. GB Skin was number one for a reason and he liked being the top dog. His products should be the best on the market and Fyra's formula would put him there—assuming it checked out like he thought it would.

Not to mention that Cass's stubbornness had piqued his.

"Threats, Gage?" Her laugh thrummed through him. "You gonna tattle to my partners about how naughty I am?"

He nearly groaned at her provocative tone.

"Nothing so pedestrian." He shifted a touch closer because he liked the scent of her, tightening the cross of his arms. Just to keep his hands where they belonged. "I wouldn't go behind your back to manipulate the other executives. This is your cross to bear, and I'm simply pointing out that you don't want this on your conscience. Do you?"

"My conscience is quite clear, thanks." Her gaze fastened firmly on his, she crossed her arms in a mirror of his pose, intentionally sliding her elbow across his. And then hung around, brushing arms deliberately. "I'll take your offer to the others. Shall I show you the way out or can you find it yourself?"

Heat flashed where they touched. "As you're late for a board meeting where I suspect one of the topics will be the offer in question, I'll see myself out."

She didn't move, still partially blocking the open doorway. On purpose. So he'd have to slide by her like he'd done when he entered the room, to show she had his number and that whatever he dished out, he should expect to have served right back. It almost pulled an appreciative chuckle out of him but he caught it at the last second. Cass had grown up in many intriguing ways and this battle was far from over.

No point in letting her believe she had a chance in hell of winning.

So close to her that he could easily see the lighter colored flecks of blue in her irises, he palmed those cutaway panels at her waist like he'd been itching to do for an eternity and drew her against him. Yes, she was still as warm as he remembered and he ached to pull the pins from her tight blond chignon to let it rain down around her shoulders.

He leaned in, nearly nuzzling her ear with his lips. Her quick intake of breath was almost as thrilling as the feel of her skin through the panels. Instead of pulling her toward him like he wanted to, he pivoted and hustled her back a step into her office.

"Tell the girls I said hi," he murmured and let her go. Though where he found the willpower, he had no idea.

She nodded, her expression blank. He was *so* going to enjoy putting a few more cracks in her newly found ice-goddess exterior when they next met.

Three

Cass blew out the breath she'd been holding. Which didn't help either her shakes or her thundering pulse.

That hadn't gone down quite like she would have hoped. She and Gage might be equals now but that hadn't afforded her any special magic to keep her insides under control.

But Gage had left and that seemed like a small win.

Except now she had to go into that board meeting, where Trinity had most definitely told the others who Cass was meeting with. So she would have to give them the whole story, including his ridiculous offer for the formula.

Of all the nerve. Telling her she owed him the formula because he'd given her a few pointers once upon a time. Oh, she owed him all right, but more like a fat lip. Fyra's success had nothing to do with Gage.

Well, the broken heart he'd left her with had driven her for a long time. But she'd succeeded by her own merit, not because he'd mentored her.

If anyone decided to sell the formula, it would be because it made sound business sense. Like she'd told him. She squared her shoulders and went to her meeting in the large, sunny room at the end of the hall.

The other three women in the C-suite ringed the conference table as the governing forces of the company they'd dubbed Fyra, from the Swedish word for four. Alex Meer ran the numbers as the chief financial officer, Dr. Harper Livingston cooked up formulas in her lab as the chief science officer, Trinity Forrester convinced consumers to buy as the chief marketing officer and Cass held the reins.

All three of her friends looked up as she entered, faces bright with expectation.

"He's gone. Let's get started." Cass set down her phone and tablet, then slid into her customary chair.

"Not so fast," Trinity said succinctly. "We've been sitting here patiently waiting for juicy details, remember?"

They'd all been friends a long time. Juicy details meant they wanted to know how she felt about seeing Gage again. Whether she wanted to punch him or just go in the corner and cry. What was he up to and had they talked about their personal lives?

She didn't have the luxury of burdening her friends with any of that because they were also her business partners. There was no room at this conference table for her emotional upheaval.

"He wants to buy Formula-47. Offered one hundred million," she said bluntly. Better to get it out on the table. "I told him it wasn't for sale. That's the extent of it."

Harper's grin slipped as she wound her strawberry blond ponytail around one finger, an absent gesture that meant her brilliant mind was blazing away. "That's hardly the extent. What's the damage? Did he hear about my formula from the trade article?"

"No." Cass hated to have to be the bearer of bad news, but they had to know. "His information was much more detailed. Which means the leak is worse than we thought."

Hearing her own words echo in her head was almost as bad as a physical blow.

"What's wrong?" Trinity asked immediately, her dark head bent at an angle as she evaluated Cass. "Did Gage get to you?"

Dang it. It had taken all of fourteen seconds for the woman who'd been Cass's best friend since eleventh grade to clue in on the undercurrents. That man had put a hitch in her stride and it was unforgivable.

"I'm concerned about the leak. That's it. Forget about Gage. I already have," she lied.

Trinity's eyes narrowed but she didn't push, thank God. Gage's timing was horrific. Why had he waltzed back into her life during such a huge professional catastrophe?

Alex, the consummate tomboy in a pair of jeans and a T-shirt, fiddled with her ever-present pen, tapping it against the legal pad on the conference table in front of her. "A hundred million is worth considering, don't you think?"

Instantly, Harper shook her head so hard, her ponytail flipped over her shoulder. Trinity and Cass scowled at Alex, who shrank under the heat of their gazes, but didn't recant her traitorous statement.

"Worth considering?" Cass's stomach contracted sharply as she took in the seriousness of Alex's expression. How could she be talking about selling so coolly? To Cass, it would be like selling her own child. "Are you out of your mind?"

"Shouldn't we consider a lucrative income stream when it's presented?" Alex argued. "We can't categorically dismiss that kind of paycheck."

They could when it was coming out of the bank account of the man who had destroyed Cass. Didn't that matter?

"Wait just a darn minute, Ms. Moneybags." Harper rounded on Alex, who shrank a bit under the redhead's scowl. "Formula-47 is my baby, not yours. I spent two years of my life perfecting it on the premise that we'd hinge our entire future strategy around the products we can create from the technology. If we sell it, we're giving up rights to it forever for a lump sum. That's not smart."

Alex tapped her pen faster against the legal pad. "Not if we retain rights and structure the deal—"

"No one is structuring deals," Cass broke in. "I only mentioned it because you needed to know. Gage's offer will vanish instantly if the leak shares the formula's recipe. And since we still don't know who it is, we have to focus on that first."

Alex firmed her mouth and nodded. "That's true."

"What did our lawyer say?" Trinity asked, raising her eyebrows as Cass blinked at her. "Didn't you just come back from Mike's office?"

"God, I'm sorry." Cass slid down in her chair an inch in mortification. Gage had wiped that entire meeting out of her head. "Mike doesn't think we can involve the police yet. The article didn't contain enough detail and wouldn't stand up in court as proprietary information. He advised us to file for FDA approval immediately, in hopes that will stem future information from being released prematurely. Until we find the leak, we can't be too careful."

She had to regain control *now*. Gage wasn't a factor. Period.

"I'm not ready." Harper shook her head mulishly. *Careful* and *thorough* might as well be tattooed on her forehead alongside her credentials, a valuable trait in a scientist who created the products with Fyra's label on them. "This is our first product that requires FDA approval. We can't rush it."

"So our lawyer gave us advice we don't plan to take." Pradas flat on the ground, Trinity leaned on the table. "What else do we have on the agenda that we need to get busy shooting down?"

"The leak is the only thing on the agenda," Cass said firmly.

Alex zeroed in on her. "What's your plan for fixing this problem, then?"

"I'm still working on it."

"You're working on it." Alex's sarcastic tone couldn't have conveyed her disbelief any more clearly. "You mean you don't have something laid out already?"

Cass froze her muscles, a trick she'd perfected over the years. She refused to let on that Alex's words had pierced her through the chest.

Alex's point wasn't lost on her. Cass should have a plan. But didn't, which was the last thing she'd admit to these women who were looking to her for leadership. "I've got some ideas. Things in the works."

"Things?" Trinity repeated incredulously.

Trinity and Alex glanced at each other and foreboding slid down Cass's spine. She was losing her edge. And everyone knew she didn't have a blessed clue how to handle this problem.

"I said I'll take care of it," Cass snapped and then immediately murmured an apology.

She couldn't believe how the meeting had deteriorated, how much it hurt to have Alex on the other side of these critical company issues. There were fractures in Fyra she hadn't known existed. Fractures in the relationships with her friends and business partners that scared her. Was

Alex disputing her ideas because she had lost confidence in Cass's ability to run Fyra?

And what was with that look Alex and Trinity had exchanged? Did they know Cass had lied about how much Gage had affected her? And Trinity hadn't defended Cass, not when Gage's offer had come up and not when Alex had attacked Cass for her lack of a plan.

It all rubbed at the raw place inside that Gage had opened up.

Cass cleared her throat and forced her CEO mask back into place. Emotions had no place in a boardroom, yet she'd been letting them run rampant thus far. It was much harder than she would have expected to shut it down given all the practice she had.

"I've got this," she said a little more calmly. "Trust me. Nothing is more important than finding this leak. Let me take care of it."

Trinity nodded. "Let's meet again on Friday. You can give us a progress report then."

Cass watched the other ladies stand and leave the conference room. No one said a word but the vote of no confidence rang out in the silence, nonetheless.

With the room empty, she let her forehead thunk the table but the wood didn't cool her raging thoughts.

She needed a plan.

But Gage had messed her up. Of course he was the reason she'd slipped up in the board meeting. Why had he picked today to dismantle her careful facade?

Her head snapped up. What if the timing wasn't coincidental? It had been bothering her how accurate his information was and how quickly on the heels of the trade article publication that he'd shown up. What if he'd planted someone in her company who was feeding him information and the mention of Fyra in the trade magazine had been designed to throw her off?

But why would he do that? He was already successful in his own right and he was willing to pay for the formula. It wasn't as if he'd put a mole in her company in hopes of stealing it.

Or was it?

She had to make sure. She'd never forgive herself if she left that stone unturned.

She also had to make progress on discovering who the culprit was and the faster the better. If the leak heard the formula was worth one hundred million dollars to GB Skin, it was as good as stolen. And Gage probably wasn't the only competitor willing to ante up.

Fyra needed Cass to step up, to lead this company. So she'd keep her friends close and her enemies closer, no matter what sort of distasteful cozying up to the CEO of GB Skin she'd have to do. After all, she *did* owe Gage Branson and it was time to pay him back.

He'd used her once upon a time. Turnabout was fair play in Gage's book, was it? It was time for Cass to wholeheartedly embrace that mantra.

Whatever Gage's game was, she'd uncover it. And maybe exact some revenge at the same time. Karma indeed.

Whistling as he rounded the Hummer's bumper, Gage went over his pitch as he strolled toward the entrance to Fyra Cosmetics only one short day after running into Cass in the parking lot. After she'd kicked him out, he'd really expected to have to push her for another appointment. When she'd called, it had been a pleasant surprise.

The 9:00 a.m. appointment had been another one. Nice to be Cass's first priority for the day. Apparently she'd thought about the logic of his offer overnight and was finally on board. Or the other executives had convinced her that selling him the formula did make for smart business, like he'd told Cass. Either way, the tide had turned.

Which was good because Arwen didn't like the hotel, and she'd let Gage know about it. Loudly. He'd have to take her on a weekend camping trip to the Hill Country to make up for all of this. Hopefully, he could melt a little of the ice in Cass's spine, close the deal and be back in Austin tomorrow.

Depending how things went with the ice melting, of course. If Cass was still as hot as he remembered under her new bulletproof CEO exterior, he might stick around for a couple of days. Arwen could rough it.

Cass didn't make him cool his heels like he'd thought she would. After yesterday, with all the power plays disguised as flirting and Cass not letting him run roughshod over her, he'd come prepared for battle. Hell, he'd kind of looked forward to another game of one-upmanship. It was rare that a woman could match him.

She appeared in the reception area looking gorgeous and untouchable in another sharp suit with a microskirt, this time in eye-popping candy pink, and she'd swept up her hair into another severe bun-like thing held by lacquered chopsticks that he immediately wanted to take apart. Why was that so hot?

He dredged up a memory of her old look from college, which had largely consisted of yoga pants and hoodies, and he'd liked that, too. But this was something else. Something elemental. He wanted to explore this new Cass in the worst way.

"Good morning, Mr. Branson," she said, though the frost in her tone told him she thought it was anything but. "This way."

The chilly greeting and use of his last name put a grin on his face. So she planned to cross swords after all. Excellent.

This time, he didn't even hesitate at the door of her office. No point in beating around the bush when the upper hand was still up for grabs. He waltzed into the middle of all that purple and plunked down into a chair. Happened to be the one behind the desk—Cass's chair—but he figured that would be enough to get her into the room.

It was. She followed him into the interior, and without batting an eye, she crossed to the desk and perched on it. Two feet from his chair. Gaze squarely on Gage, she crossed her stocking-clad legs with a slow and deliberate slide and let her stilettos dangle. The little skirt rode up her thighs almost to the point of indecency.

His tongue went numb as all the blood rushed from his head, pooling into a spectacular hard-on. One tiny push with his heel and Cass's chair would roll him into a proximity much better suited to enjoying the smorgasbord of delights inches away.

This was his punishment for stealing her chair? She clearly didn't get how corporate politics, particularly between competitors, worked.

"Thanks for coming on short notice," she purred and the subtle innuendo wasn't lost on him.

"Thanks for having me," he returned and cleared the rasp from his throat. Maybe she knew a little more about this game than he'd supposed. "You ready to talk details?"

"Sure, if you want to jump right into it." She cocked her head, watching him. "The others don't want to sell. But I'm willing to talk to them."

Instantly suspicious, he grinned and crossed his arms, leaning back in the chair so he could see all of her at once. She was something else. "Along with what strings?"

"Oh, nothing much." She waved a French-manicured hand airily and leaned forward, one palm on the desk. Her silky button-up shirt billowed a bit, just enough to draw his attention to her cleavage but not enough to actually show anything.

The anticipation of catching a glimpse of skin had his mouth watering.

"Name your price, Cass," he murmured and wondered what she'd do if he pulled her off that desk into his lap. "I'm assuming one hundred million wasn't enough?"

"Not quite. You also have to help me catch the leak first."

His gaze snapped back up to her beautiful face as her meaning registered. "Help you catch the leak? You mean you haven't already?"

Unacceptable. Hadn't she learned anything important from him? Yesterday he sure would have said so, but obviously she needed a few more pointers about how to run her business.

"I have a plan," she explained calmly. "And you're it. Until the leak is stopped, Fyra can't make a major decision like selling our formula. Surely you understand that."

He did. This was a wrinkle he hadn't anticipated. But what she was proposing—it meant he'd have to stay in Dallas longer than he'd anticipated. He ran a successful company, too, and it was suffering from his lack of attention. If he stayed, he'd have to ship Arwen home, which she'd never forgive him for.

"You should have already handled the leak," he groused.

"I know."

Her voice didn't change. Her expression didn't change. But something shifted as he realized how hard this conversation was for her. She hadn't wanted to admit that.

Disturbed at the sudden revelation, he stared at her and

his heart thumped strangely. He'd been so busy examining the angles, he'd failed to see this was actually just a baseline plea for help that she'd disguised well.

"Work with me, Gage. Together, like old times."

She wanted to pick up where they left off. Maybe in more ways than one. The simple phrases reached out and grabbed hold of his lungs. It echoed through his mind, his chest, and the thought pleased him. Enormously.

It was a redo of college, where he was her mentor and she soaked it all up like a sponge with a side of hero worship that made him feel invincible. That had been a heady arrangement for a twenty-four-year-old. But they weren't kids anymore.

And he didn't for a moment underestimate Cass. She'd suggested this for some reason he couldn't figure out yet. Which didn't keep him from contemplating that redo. Who was he kidding? He'd wanted her the moment he'd turned around in the parking lot yesterday and gotten an eyeful of grown-up Cass. If he hung around and helped her, it gave him an opportunity to get her naked again.

And he could ensure the problem with the leak was handled like it should have been from the get-go. Not to mention he could dig a bit to uncover her real motives here.

Her eyes huge and warm, she watched him and he was lost. Dang. She'd played this extremely well. There was absolutely no way he could say no. He didn't want to say no.

But a yes didn't mean he'd do it without adding a few strings of his own.

"I'll help you. Until Sunday. I have a meeting Monday that can't be rescheduled."

Her smile hit him crossways. And then it slipped from her face as he leaned forward oh-so-slowly. Mute, she stared at his hand as he braced it on the desk a millimeter from her thigh. He could slip a finger right under the hem of that tiny skirt. And his mind got busy on imagining where that would lead.

"But you have to do something for me," he murmured. He got as close to her as he dared, crowding her space where all the trappings of business melted away and they were simply man and woman.

She smelled classy and expensive, and instantly he wanted that scent on his own skin, transferred by her body heat as she writhed under him. He could lean her back against that desk and at this angle, the pleasure would be intense. The image made him a little lightheaded as his erection intensified.

"I already said I'd talk to the others about selling you the formula," she said a touch breathlessly, but to her credit, she didn't allow one single muscle twitch to give away whether she welcomed his nearness or preferred the distance. "*If* we catch the leak."

That ice-goddess routine needed to go, fast. That wasn't going to happen here. Not under these circumstances. If he wanted to take things to the next level, he had to go bold or go home.

"Yes, but you're doing that because deep down, you know you owe me. If I help you find the leak, you owe me again. Turnabout, sweetheart."

"What do you want?"

Oh, where should I start? "Nothing you can't handle."

The knowing glint in her gaze said she already had a pretty good idea what gauntlet he was about to throw down. They stared at each other for a long moment and her breathing hitched as he reached out and slid a thumb along her jawline.

"You have to take me to dinner."

Four

Cass's laughter bubbled to the surface in spite of it all. Gingerly she dabbed at her eyes without fear thanks to Harper's smudge-proof mascara. "That's what you want? Dinner?"

She'd been braced for...anything but that. Especially since she had the distinct impression he was working as many angles as she was.

His fingers dropped away, but her face was still warm where he'd stroked her. She missed his touch instantly.

Why had she thought sitting on the desk would give her an edge? Seemed so logical before she actually did it. Gage had taken her chair in deliberate provocation that she absolutely couldn't ignore. So she'd trapped him behind the desk and put all her good stuff at eye level. It should have been the perfect distraction. For *him*. The perfect way to spend the entire conversation looking down at him, imagining that he was suffering over her brilliant strategic move.

Karma, baby.

Instead, she'd spent half of the conversation acutely aware that all her good stuff was at eye level. He'd noticed, quite appreciatively, and it hit her in places she'd forgotten that felt so good when heated by a man's interest.

The other half of the conversation had been spent trying to stay one step ahead of Gage while feeding him the right combination of incentives to get him to agree to help. If he was up to no good, what better way to keep tabs on him than under the guise of working together to uncover the source of the leak? Besides, she hadn't done so hot at resolving the leak on her own. If they kept their activities on the down-low, no one had to know she'd outsourced the problem.

If they caught the leak—*and* Gage wasn't involved— she'd absolutely talk to the other girls about selling the formula. She hadn't specified what she'd say…but she'd talk to them all right. The conversation might be more along the lines of no way in hell she'd sell, but he didn't have to know that.

It was a win-win for everyone.

Crossing his heart with one lazy finger, he grinned. "Totally serious."

"Dinner?" She pretended to contemplate. "Like a date?"

"Not *like* a date. A date. And you're paying."

A God-honest date? The idea buzzed around inside, looking for a place to land, sounding almost…nice. She'd love to have dinner over a glass of wine with an interesting man who looked at her like Gage was looking at her right now.

She shook it off. She couldn't go on a real date with Gage Branson. It was ludicrous. The man was a heartbreaker of the highest order.

Instead, she should be thinking of how a date fell in

line with her strategy. A little after-hours party, just the two of them. Some drinks and a few seductive comments and, oh, look. Gage slips and says something incriminating, like the name of the person he'd planted at her company. The one who was feeding him information he could use to his advantage.

And she would pretend she wasn't sad it had to be this way.

Coy was the way to go here. But she had to tread very carefully with the devil incarnate. No point in raising his suspicions by agreeing to his deal right out of the gate. "What if I already have plans for dinner tonight?"

She *did* have plans. If working until everyone else left and then going home to her empty eight-thousand-square-foot house on White Rock Lake, where she'd open a bottle of wine and eat frozen pizza, counted as plans.

"Cancel them," he ordered. "You're too busy worrying about the leak to have fun, anyway. Have dinner with someone who gets that. Where you can unload and unwind without fear."

"What makes you think I need to unwind?" she purred to cover the sudden catch in her throat. Had she tipped him off somehow that she was tense and frantic 24/7?

His slow smile irritated her. How dare he get to her?

"Oh, I'm practicing my mindreading skills," he told her blithely. "I see that things are rough around here. You can't be happy that word got out about your unreleased formula. You're at a unique place in your career where you have millions of dollars and a large number of people's jobs at stake. You want to keep it all together and convince everyone that you have things under control. With me, you don't have to. I get it."

Something inside crumbled under his assessment.

Guess that shield she'd thought she'd developed wasn't so effective after all. How was he still so good at reading her?

Now would be a good time for that distance she should have put between them long ago. She unglued herself from the desk and rounded it, an ineffective barrier against the open wounds in her chest but better than nothing. Let him make what he chose out of her move.

"You can't come in here and throw around pop psychology," she told him, pleased how calmly she delivered it. "You don't know anything about me, Gage. Not anymore."

Arms crossed, he watched her from behind her own desk, still wearing a faint trace of that smile. "Yet you didn't say I was wrong."

She shut her eyes for a beat. Dinner was going to be far more difficult than she'd anticipated.

If Gage was involved in corporate espionage, catching him in the act was the only way to prove to the others she could lead Fyra through these difficult circumstances. Plus it got rid of him, once and for all. His hundred-million-dollar offer wouldn't be a factor and the leak would be stopped.

He'd get exactly what he deserved.

Then she could get started on getting over him—for real, this time. She could stop hating him. And stop being affected by him. And stop turning down every man who asked her out. The chaos inside with Gage's name written all over it had driven her for so long. Wasn't it time to move on? That was what *she* deserved.

"I'm not what you'd call a fun date," she said. "I have a very boring life outside of these walls. Dinner is a chance to discuss the leak. Strictly business."

A token protest. She knew good and well it was anything but.

"Is that really what you want, Cass?" he asked softly,

as if he already knew the answer. "Because it sounds to me as if you need a friend."

Of all the things she'd thought he come back with, that was not one of them. The laugh escaped her clamped lips before she could catch it. "What, like you're volunteering? I have lots of friends, thanks."

But did she really? This time last week, she would have said Trinity would take a bullet for her. They'd been friends for almost fifteen years. It still stung that no one had stood up for Cass in the board meeting, but Trinity's silence had hurt the worst.

Alex's defection was almost as bad.

Cass and Alex had met in a freshman-level algebra class. It had taken Cass four months to convince Alex she had what it took to be the CFO of a multimillion-dollar corporation and Cass had been right. Alex's lack of confidence and all the talk of selling hurt.

Cass was afraid the cracks in Fyra's foundation were really cracks in *her* foundation. The last person she could stomach finding out about the division in Fyra was Gage Branson, and it would be just like him to sniff out her weaknesses.

So she wouldn't show him any.

"There's always room for one more friend," Gage countered softly. "In fact, I changed my mind. Let *me* take *you* to dinner and you can relax for a while. Wear a dress and we'll leave our titles at the door."

There he went again, working his magic because that sounded like the exact date she'd envisioned. He was the last man on earth she should be envisioning it with, though. "How do you know that's what I need?"

"Cass. I know you. You can't have changed too much over the years. At least I hope you haven't."

Before she could figure out how to respond to that, he

rounded the desk and took her hand to hold it tight in his surprisingly smooth one. For a guy who'd always spent a lot of time outdoors, his skin should be rougher. It was a testament to GB Skin and the effectiveness of his products that it wasn't.

She stared at his chiseled jaw, gorgeous hazel eyes and beautiful face framed by the longish brown hair he'd always favored and something unhitched in her chest.

Gage had broken her so thoroughly because she'd once given this man her soul.

That hadn't been an accident. A mistake, surely, but not because she didn't realize what she was doing. She'd fallen in love with Gage willingly. He'd filled her, completely. Because he understood her, believed in her. Taught her, pushed her, stimulated her.

All of it rushed back and she went a little dizzy with the memories of what had been holy and magnificent about their relationship.

"Say yes," he prompted, squeezing her hand. "I promise not to mention how boring you are."

Despite everything, she laughed, oddly grateful that he had figured out how to get her to.

"Yes," she said. There'd really never been another choice. "But we split the check."

He couldn't be allowed to affect her. The good stuff about their relationship didn't matter because at the end of the day, Gage didn't do commitment and never would.

"That part's nonnegotiable," he said with a wicked smile. "I'm paying. After all, I bullied you into it."

Mission accomplished. He had no clue he'd spent this entire conversation persuading her into exactly what she wanted to do. For that alone, she returned the smile. "You haven't seen the price of the obscenely expensive wine I plan to order."

"I'll pick you up at eight," he said, clearly happy to have gotten what he wanted, though why he considered dinner such a coup was beyond her. He had an angle here that she hadn't yet discovered.

She watched him leave. That gave her nearly ten hours to figure out how to keep Gage at arm's length while cozying up to him. Hours she'd use to figure out how to pump him for information while keeping him in the dark about her motives.

Ten hours to figure out how to seduce answers out of Gage Branson without falling for him all over again. All she had to do was focus on his sins and the rest would be a walk in the park.

Gage knocked on Cass's door at seven fifty-five.

Nice place. A bit too glass-and-steel for his tastes but Cass's house overlooked a big lake with a walking trail around it. His own house in Austin was near a lake. Funny how their tastes in views had aligned all these years later.

She swung open the door wearing a sheer lacy dress that hugged her body in all the right places. Cranberry-colored, which was somehow ten times racier than red would have been, it rendered him speechless. When he'd told her to wear a dress, he'd fully expected her to wear anything but.

His body sprang to full attention. He could not get a handle on her.

"You're early," she said with an amused brow lift. "I like an eager man."

The blood that should have been stimulating his brain into a snappy response seemed to have vacated for a warmer locale in the south.

Cass wasn't a college student any longer. Not that he was confused. But he was having a hard time reconciling how *much* she'd changed. Cassandra Claremont, CEO, might be the most intriguing woman on the planet. She was also far more of a challenge because she seemed to have developed Gage-proof armor.

Dinner was supposed to level the playing field. Warm up that ice so he could get her used to the idea of selling him the formula because she recognized what she owed him. She might be willing to talk to the other ladies about the formula, but he needed her to convince them, not talk about it. For that, she had to be totally in his corner. How was he supposed to get her there when he couldn't get his feet under himself long enough to figure out what game she was playing?

"Uh…" *Brain not engaging.* He shook off the Cass stupor. "It's only early if you're more than fifteen minutes ahead. Technically, I'm right on time."

"Where are you taking me for dinner, Mr. Right-on-Time?" She cocked her head, sending her dangly diamond earrings dancing.

His body was not interested in food. At all.

"I'll let you choose," he allowed magnanimously. "Since you cancelled your previous plans."

Not for the first time, he wondered what she'd told the poor schmuck she'd ditched, who'd likely spent all day anticipating his date with Cass. Had she admitted to her date that an old boyfriend had unexpectedly come to town? A business deal had suddenly fallen in her lap that she needed to attend to? She had to wash her hair?

It probably didn't matter. She'd be forgiven for breaking the date regardless. Cass was a gorgeous, sophisticated woman who ran a multimillion dollar company and she likely had her pick of companions. Suave execs, successful doctors, cut athletes with Pro-Bowl or all-star credentials. The dating circles were wide open and she was most definitely sleeping with *someone*. A woman like Cass wouldn't be alone except by choice.

That burn in your gut? Feels a lot like jealousy.

Ridiculous. So Nicolas didn't get it right *all* the time.

Gage and Cass hadn't been an item for nearly a decade. Sure, he'd thought about her and wondered what might have been if he wasn't so averse to being tied down, but he hadn't spent all his nights alone since then either. Though lately, a couple of hours at the dog park with Arwen was more fun than wading through the pool of women in his circle. That was the one downside to guarding your freedom so ferociously—you went through eligible women pretty quickly.

"That's so generous of you to let me pick after leaving me so few choices otherwise," she said, infusing it with enough sarcasm to clue him in that she still wasn't clear on what she owed him.

"You always have choices," he countered. "One just might lead to a different place than the other."

"Well said." With a cryptic nod, she brushed past him onto the front steps, engulfing him in a delicious haze of jasmine and other exotic spices. On Cass, the scent was half "come and get me" and half "I'm untouchable." A thoroughly arousing combination.

Somehow, he managed to drive to the restaurant without veering off into a ditch. Or a shadowy hiding place between two buildings where he could ravish the cool beauty in the next seat. If he wanted her willing, he had to get back on track. But the ice in her spine seemed extra hard and cold tonight.

The restaurant was as highbrow as they came, making him glad he'd tossed a suit in his overnight bag, just in case. The maître d' led them to a secluded table in the

back, exactly as Gage had instructed, and left them bless-
edly alone.

Except Gage still didn't know how to play this dinner.
Seduction or strategy? Which would get him an invitation through the front door of Cass's house at the end of
the night? Because seduction might be the only way to get
what he wanted in the end. A sated Cass might make for
a much more reasonable Cass. But they did need to work
together on the leak or the formula would be worthless.
He couldn't ignore the need to discuss strategy.

Fortunately, what he apparently lacked in ESP, he made
up for in charm and ingenuity. So he'd wing it. Like always.

Gage barely glanced at the wine menu before handing
it over to Cass. "Since you called dibs on ordering the
wine, here you go."

She arched one of those cool brows and took the leather-
bound wine listing. The movement drew attention to her
cleavage, where scarcely-contained nipples threatened to
burst free of their cranberry lace cage at a moment's notice. A bead of sweat slid between his shoulder blades as
he tore his gaze from her breasts.

"I was expecting more of an argument," she commented as if the sexual undercurrents didn't exist. "You're
not a fan of wine, if memory serves."

No, but the fact that she recalled his preference put a
good deal more warmth down south. As if he'd had room
for more.

"I'll make an exception for you."

The more she drank, the less she'd remember to act like
the ice goddess, or at least that had been the plan once
upon a time when his faculties were in order. Back in her
office, she'd seemed…brittle. As if she'd needed someone

to pay attention to her. Cass was in sore need of a glass of wine and an orgasm, and not necessarily in that order.

That made up his mind. He wanted to give her a chance to relax, as he'd entreated her to. One of them should be able to anyway. Seduction first. And then they could talk leak strategy later. Much later.

With their food, Cass ordered a four hundred dollar bottle of wine—exorbitant, as promised—and once the waiter left to retrieve it, she folded her hands, contemplating Gage as if she'd found an amusing little puppy she didn't know whether to pet or send outside for peeing on the floor.

"Tell me something," she began in her boardroom voice that he should not find so sexy.

"Sure. I'm an open book." He spread his hands wide, earning a small, less-than-amused smile. She needed to drink more. Maybe her Gage-proof armor would fall off along with her inhibitions.

Once, they'd talked about everything under the sun and he'd enjoyed hearing her thoughts and soothing her through her angst. Just like he'd enjoyed being her mentor, shaping her, guiding her.

Maybe you hope to fall into that role again, with the hero worship and Pygmalion overtones, hmm?

Yeah. He did. And she needed his help to find the leak. Needed *him*. So what? Seduction *and* strategy, then. All of that worked together to get him the formula. Where was the harm?

"Why the interest in my formula?" she asked point-blank. "Other than the song and dance about how I owe it to you. For real. Why? You've expanded your retail reach enormously over the past five years and you just landed that endorsement deal. Something must have prompted you to show up on my doorstep."

"That's a fair question," he acknowledged, impressed that she'd done her homework on his company. And that's why he chose to answer her honestly. "It's simple really. My target consumers are starting to pay close attention to things like bar-fight scars and wrinkles. So I launched my own product. I don't want any competition."

"Gage, there are a hundred wrinkle creams on the market. Your competition is legion."

"No." He caught her gaze and held it. "There's only one person who's my equal."

"So this is a pride thing." Looking away, she sipped the glass of wine the waiter had placed in front of her and murmured her appreciation for the red blend. "You can't stand it when a competitor is primed to beat you."

He might as well be made of glass when it came to Cass and that was sexy, too. Dang if he could figure out why he was so drawn to her when all he should care about was whatever got him that formula.

Ignoring his own vile glass of headache in a bottle, he grinned because it would be pointless to argue when she clearly saw the truth. But that didn't mean they had to dwell on it.

Gage slid a palm across the table and captured her hand before she could prevent it. "Don't think of me as your competition, not tonight."

She glanced down at their joined hands but didn't snatch hers away. He could tell she was contemplating it, though, hopefully because she also felt the electricity between them—and it was working to loosen her up.

"But you are. Always and forever. We sell similar products or you wouldn't be here. Nor would you have been my mentor. Competition is not something you can will away."

"Maybe not. I can, however, ban all business talk until later. Then we're just old friends reconnecting. Like I told you in your office."

He had the distinct impression she didn't loosen up easily these days. If there was any competition going on tonight, that was it. And he didn't intend to lose this particular contest.

"I'm curious," she said, her gaze back on him but not nearly warm enough for his taste. "I never see you at trade shows. My email address is easy to locate on Fyra's website. If you have such an interest in reconnecting, why haven't we done so before now?"

A hot prickle walked across the back of his neck as he instantly recognized a spring-loaded trap, ready to close around his leg if he moved the wrong way. An unsettled feeling bled through his chest.

And in the end, *he* was the one to pull his hand back from hers, suddenly uncomfortable with the contact.

"I hate trade shows. They're stifling. And they're always on weekends when I'm…busy."

That had sounded much dirtier than he'd intended, especially when lately, his weekends had consisted of giving Arwen a bath or taking her to the lake so she could have fun practicing her pointer skills.

Cass watched him without blinking, silently waiting on him to stop stalling and get to the meat of her question, which was basically designed to force him to admit he'd developed an interest in her in order to get his hands on her formula.

Maybe it had started out as a little of both—seducing her to ensure she remembered what she owed him. He wasn't a saint.

But at this moment, he really did want to be a friend. None of her other so-called friends seemed to realize how brittle she was under her super-CEO costume. Someone had to banish the shadows of fatigue and uncertainty in her gaze. Give her a safe place to let her hair down, which would preferably be in his bed, like she'd once done.

Yeah. He'd like to pull those pins from the tight blond twist at her crown, all right. His lower half went rock solid as he imagined that fall of hair raining down around her bare shoulders as he peeled that lacy, sexy cranberry-colored dress from her beautiful body. It was crazy to be so hot for her again after not seeing her for so long—or to her point, after not actively pursuing reacquaintance for all these years.

He should have looked her up. Why hadn't he?

He blew out a pent-up breath. "Truth? I didn't drive up from Austin to reconnect over a drink. I want your formula. But that's just business."

Tonight was very personal.

Nodding at the wine bottle, she drained her glass and held it out for Gage to pour her another. "I'm surprised you'd admit it."

"I told you, I'm an open book. I don't mind being cagey when the occasion calls for it, but I don't have deep dark secrets." Who had time for that noise? Life was too short to care about other people's opinions, and that's all secrets were—things you didn't want others to know because you feared their judgment.

Cass leaned forward and the new angle did fascinating things to the deep V over her breasts. Not that he was a lecher, but come on. A lady didn't wear a dress like that if she didn't want her date to notice her spectacular breasts. And a lady who didn't want a man to imagine tasting her breasts definitely didn't *lean*.

"Really. No secrets?"

"Really, really." His tongue was still a bit thick.

"Sounds like we need to play a game of truth or dare, then."

Five

Cass held her breath as Gage's gaze flew to hers. It had been lingering somewhere in the vicinity of her cleavage, and the heat from his appreciation had been warming her uncomfortably for the better part of ten minutes. But what had she expected with such a daring wardrobe choice?

Gage's eyes on her body were far more affecting than any other man's hands would be.

Question marks shooting from the top of his head, Gage lifted a brow. "Yeah, truth or dare. That's what I was thinking, too. How did you know?"

She bit back the laugh. Even when he was being sarcastic, he was still charming. She wasn't falling for it. "I'm serious. If you don't have any secrets, should be an easy game."

And she could pump him for information about his involvement in the leak without raising red flags. It was brilliant.

Lazily he traced the rim of his untouched wineglass, watching her with undisguised calculation. But what all those equations added up to, she had no idea. The clink of silverware against china filled the sudden silence, along with snatches of conversation from other diners.

"You know how that game works, right?" he finally asked.

She waved dismissively. "Of course, or I wouldn't have suggested it. I ask you a question and if you don't choose to answer it honestly, you have to do whatever I dare you to."

"And you have to do the same." The once-over he slid down her body unleashed a shiver.

She'd considered that. Not enough, apparently. "Yeah, so? I'm not worried."

The waiter brought their dinners but instead of picking up a fork, Gage folded his hands in front of his plate of salmon and asparagus. "You probably should be. But now I'm insanely curious what you want to know that you feel you have to bury inside a game. You could just ask."

Her pulse tripped as she scrambled for a response. She was slipping. How had he seen through that ploy so *easily*? "That's no fun."

His laugh curled up inside her thickly. "It *so* can be, but it's all in the asking. No matter. I'm in. Truth or dare away. Truth for my first round."

Forking a bite of salmon into his mouth, he watched her expectantly and it bobbled her pulse again. This was why she sold cosmetics for a living instead of becoming an investigator. There was a skill to it apparently, one that she lacked. Too late to back out now.

"Have you ever…" She cursed silently. Thinking on the fly was one of her strong suits but not with Gage's hazel laser beams boring into her. *Say something.* "Cheated on your taxes?"

"That's your question?" He shook his head with a laugh. "I'm almost afraid to ask what the dare would be. But it doesn't matter because I have nothing to hide. As much as I think the corporate tax structure needs to be reworked in favor of businesses, no, I've never cheated on my taxes."

Taxes. Could she be more boring? Despite having warned him that she was not a fun date, she had a goal here and she needed to get on it by steering the conversation toward his ethics. "But you cheat at cards. All the time."

His slow smile did something X-rated to her insides. "That's only when we're playing strip poker, darling. And believe me, it's worth it."

The memory of messing around in college, using things like card games as foreplay, spiked through her. They'd always ended up naked and breathless. The anticipation had been drawn out over the length of a game she could hardly pay attention to because Gage had been revealing himself oh-so-slowly while she sat there in a similar state of vulnerability.

Kind of like now.

And she couldn't unthink it. Back then, when they'd finally come together, she'd exploded under his careful and thorough lovemaking. Because he had always thoroughly engaged her—mind, body and soul.

And that hadn't changed. The moment she'd recognized Gage in the parking lot, it felt as though she'd woken up from a coma. She hadn't realized how much she'd missed being so comprehensively engaged. How much she missed a man paying attention to her.

No. Not any man. This one.

Their gazes met over the table, burning up the atmosphere. Obviously he was recalling their hot and heavy times, as well, and his expression unleashed a shiver she couldn't control. Something unknitted inside, falling apart as if all the glue holding her together melted at Gage-point-five degrees.

They'd once been so close because they had so much in common. They'd shared the same goals, and she'd always been able to count on him to have the answers she sought. She'd counted on him to encourage her, to push her. Because he understood her.

It was so much more powerful now that they were equals. Gage Branson, CEO, was so much more attractive than he'd been as her mentor.

Fork suspended in midair, he tilted his head. "Weren't we playing a game?"

Cass blinked. The game. The suspicions. Her precarious position within Fyra. She bit back an unladylike swear word and took a fortifying sip of wine.

How had she fallen into Gage so easily that she'd forgotten what this dinner was supposed to be about? He'd cursed her with his magic voice and wicked personality, lulling her into believing they were former lovers reconnecting over a drink.

He wasn't on her side, not like he used to be. Maybe he never had been. As he was making love to her, he'd probably already be plotting his escape. Just like he'd almost assuredly plotted to steal her formula.

Gage Branson, CEO, wasn't any more of a good bet with her heart than he had been as a graduate student.

She steeled her spine against the good memories and dredged up the bad ones. She'd spent years working sixteen-hour days so she could fall into bed exhausted and actually sleep. Otherwise, she lay there in misery, aching over having lost the love of her life.

And here he was again, ripe for a comeuppance and

deserving of whatever she threw at him. She narrowed her gaze and shoved back the past. "We got off track. Sorry. Next question. Have you ever stolen anything?"

"I'm supposed to say whether I want truth or dare first." Warily, he eyed her. "What's with all these moral questions anyway? Admittedly, it's been a long time since I played truth or dare, but I seem to recall we always asked things like who was your first crush or have you ever gone skinny-dipping?"

"Those are great questions for eleven-year-olds. This is the adult version," she informed him pertly and was instantly sorry as something wicked flashed through his expression.

"Why didn't you say so?" His slow smile had all sorts of danger signs attached to it. "I'd like to take the dare, then."

She cursed. *Should have anticipated that he'd take the dare, dummy.* "I dare you to answer the question."

"Oh, no, honey," he said with a laugh. "It doesn't work like that. You promised me the adult version and I'm fully prepared to pay up for not answering. Lay it on me."

Clearly he expected the dare to come packaged in a thinly veiled sexual wrapper. So she indulged him with a sensuous smile. "I dare you to take your shirt off."

"Here?" He glanced around the crowded, high-class restaurant with a dubious line between his brows. "It doesn't seem fair to show up all these other guys. Can't you think of something else?"

Typical male machismo. Of course if his body still looked like it used to—and chances were high that it did—his point was valid.

"Chicken?" she asked sweetly. "You wanted the dare."

"I'd be happy to take my shirt off," he growled. "In the car. In your living room. In your office. No card game required. Pick another locale, sweetheart, and dare me to get naked to your heart's content. Unfortunately, there are both a dress code and health regulations in a restaurant. Which means your dare is invalid."

First the insistence he always paid his fair share of taxes and then he'd refused her dare because of *health regulations*? She bit back the noise of disgust. Barely. "When did you become such a boy scout?"

"I've never willingly broken the law." He shrugged. "So there's your answer since I can't take the dare. My turn."

"Your turn for what?" she asked, temporarily distracted by his claim to be a law-abiding citizen.

Honesty? Just because truth was the name of the game didn't mean he wasn't lying. But in reality, he'd never been anything but forthright in their relationship. Sure, he'd dumped her and broken her heart. But he'd been honest about it.

"To ask you a question." He finished off his dinner and chewed thoughtfully. "What's the name of the last guy you were in love with?"

Love. The word echoed through her chest cavity, which was still empty thanks to the last guy she'd fallen in love with. Her stomach rolled and the wine soured in her mouth.

Stupid game. She could lie. But he'd see through that as though he was reading her mind. And she couldn't take the dare—she'd bet his hundred million it would be something impossible like sit in his lap for five minutes or put her underwear in his pocket with her toes.

Why had she started this game? To prove he'd become someone untrustworthy, when she had no evidence of his involvement in the leak? To prove she wasn't affected by him any longer, when she'd only managed to prove the exact opposite?

Or some deeper reason that she couldn't admit, even internally?

Trapped and furious with herself, she stared at him as her frustration grew. And then she pictured the shock on his face if she blurted out *Gage Branson* in response to his question. That was perhaps what stung the most—he didn't even realize he'd detonated a landmine in her heart.

The emotional agitation inside boiled over. And that was unacceptable.

"Excuse me." She threw her napkin into the middle of her plate of uneaten chicken marsala and fled to the bathroom before the sob beating in her throat escaped.

What in the... Gage watched Cass do the hundred-yard sprint through the obstacle course of tables and waiters, presumably headed for the restrooms at the rear of the building.

She'd started this silly game. Was she really that upset he hadn't taken her dare? Why—because she wanted him naked and was too afraid to come right out and say it?

He shook his head and thought seriously about draining his untouched glass of wine to see if Cass made any more sense when he had a buzz. The subsequent headache would at least be more easily explained than the one Cass was giving him.

She didn't return for a long while. A little concerned, Gage followed her, hoping to find a female employee to check on her if need be. Except she was sitting on the velvet bench at the end of the long hallway, her vibe so edgy, he could almost feel the tension.

"Hey," he said softly as he approached. "What's up? Trying to skip out on me? I said I'd pay."

The joke didn't get the smile he'd hoped for. In fact, her expression remained completely blank. "I'm fine."

"Yeah. I can see that." Taking a chance that she'd welcome the company, he sat on the bench next to her.

She didn't move. He'd noticed she did that a lot, holding herself frozen. But this time, he was close enough to see the muscle spasms in her thighs as if she was fighting her body's natural instincts to flee in some kind of mind-over-matter contest.

"I'm sorry I didn't play the game fairly," he said sincerely. And gingerly, in case that wasn't the reason she was upset. Women and emotions were not his forte and he wouldn't be surprised to learn this was one of those situations where if he didn't know why she was upset— she sure wasn't going to tell him.

"You did." She stared straight ahead. "I'm the one who was playing unfairly. You were right, the dare wasn't valid."

Somehow, her admission of guilt managed to sound as if she felt it was anything but her fault. Which was a rare talent.

"Okay. You ready to get out of here, then?" He nodded toward the end of the hallway. "Or do you want to finish dinner?"

"What would be the point of finishing dinner?" she asked in a monotone that pricked the hair on the back of his neck.

This strange mood went well beyond her normal reserve. When he'd labeled her demeanor as *brittle* earlier, he'd had no clue how much more so she could actually become, as if he had to watch how heavily he breathed for fear of shattering her into a million pieces.

"The point of dinner is so I can spend time with you," he said. And…some other agenda items that had somehow slipped his mind in favor of the woman herself.

That earned him a sidelong glance. "I told you I wasn't a fun date."

"I'm having fun," he told her automatically and then had to clarify. "Well, I *was*. And then you disappeared."

Physically and mentally.

"That was fun?" She tilted her head toward the dining room, her eyes incredulously wide. "I made you drink wine, which you hate, and then foisted a teenagers' sleepover game on you. Which part did you find the most entertaining?"

"All of it." He grinned in spite of her mood and accepted her scowl with a nod. "You heard me. I have legs and I know how to use them. Trust me, I've got no problem walking out of a restaurant in the middle of a date. I don't waste my time on things that aren't fun."

"Really?"

"Honesty. It isn't just for breakfast anymore."

And finally, he scored a small laugh. Why did that make his chest feel so tight and full?

"I guess I'm done with dinner." She sneaked another glance at him and he pretended not to notice.

"But not with spending time together?" He resisted the urge to reach out. He wanted to touch her but he couldn't gauge if her mood had shifted enough to welcome it.

"Well…" She crossed her arms, hiding her hands underneath, as if she'd sensed that he'd been contemplating taking one of them. "We were supposed to be talking about the leak. I think we have to do that together."

Which wasn't an answer at all. "You know dinner wasn't about the leak. Don't be dense."

"I was giving you the benefit of the doubt," she countered. "I'm well aware that you're playing all the angles."

And that was the opportunity he'd been waiting for. Since her hands were still locked behind the cross of her arms, he opted to slide one chunk of hair from her cheek and lingered at her neck. Touching that beautiful alabaster skin had suddenly grown more important than breathing. So he indulged himself, letting his fingers play with her neck. And then he tipped her head back so he could meet her gaze.

A shield snapped over her expression. That look he recognized. The ice goddess returneth. Excellent. Now he could get started melting her, like he'd planned. Though the reasons that had felt so necessary at the beginning of the night weren't the same as they were now. At all.

"No angles," he murmured and drew her face closer. Almost within kissing distance. But not quite. "I asked you to dinner because I wanted to. You…interest me. I want to find out how you've changed since college. Discover what's still the same."

Cass didn't look away, challenging him with merely the glint in her eye. "So you can use it to your advantage."

God, that was sexy. In-charge, take-no-prisoners Cass was something else. His motor started humming. "Absolutely. I fully intend to use every scrap of information I learn to seduce you."

Not even a blink to show she'd registered that he'd shifted away from business and zeroed in on pleasure. Which was where they'd keep it if he had his way. Oh, he'd eventually wind his way back to the formula. But for now, it was all about Cass.

"I think you've forgotten that I specified this dinner should be strictly business. I was about to thank you for sticking to it."

Ah-ha. Her voice had grown a little huskier and it skated through his blood, raising the heat a notch. She wasn't as unaffected as she wanted him to believe.

"Sorry," he apologized without a shred of regret. "I

never agreed to that. But we're smart people. We can keep business and pleasure separate. Like we did in college."

He watched her expression smooth out, becoming blank. Which meant he'd hit a nerve.

"I can," she said firmly. "I'm not so sure about you."

"I'm good for it." *Press your advantage. Now.* "If you are, too, prove it."

Her gaze dropped to his mouth. "How?"

Heat and awareness shot through the roof. God, that dress clung to her curves like a second skin. Would it be terrible if he hooked both sleeves with his thumbs and yanked it down so he could feast his eyes on her beautiful bare breasts?

Gage tipped her chin up with a crooked finger to bring her mouth in range. But he didn't take it with his. Not yet.

"So, let me see if I've got this straight," Cass murmured, her breath mingling with his. "By your logic, if I kiss you, that'll prove I can separate business from pleasure?"

"Who said anything about kissing?" he countered. "Is that what's on your mind, Cass? Because I'm game if you think kissing me will make your point."

It was a dare and a challenge—guaranteed to get an in-control, powerful woman like Cass hot—and she caught both full force. Her mouth curved upward as she contemplated him. "I think it'll make your point, not mine."

"Oh?" Barely six inches separated their lips and he ached to close that distance. "What point is that?"

She leaned in, almost there but not quite, lips feathering against his, and it was more evocative than if she'd gone for it. Her perfume engulfed him in a sensuous wave that heightened the sparking awareness. Her breasts brushed his chest aggressively and he nearly groaned with the effort it took to keep his fingers from her dress.

One little signal and he'd slide his arms around her, pulling her into the fiercest kiss. The only prayer he had of cracking that ice was to give her something sizzling hot to grab on to with both hands.

Public place, public place, public place, he reminded himself furiously.

"Your point—if I recall—was that you'd use all the information at your disposal to seduce me," she murmured throatily. "I don't think you have a shot."

"Guess there's only one way to find out."

The irresistible draw between them sucked him in, and finally his arms closed around her and her mouth sought his. A scorching kiss ignited the pent-up emotions and desire Gage had been fighting since he'd first laid eyes on Cass in the parking lot of her building.

They twined together, shifting closer. As close as they could on the bench without turning the kiss into something too indecent for public consumption.

Yes. Oh, God yes. Her tongue darted out in a quest for his and he lost himself in the sensation of her hot flesh. She tasted of wine and familiarity, throwing him back to a time when she'd been a major part of his first round of freedom.

Memories zipped by of Cass spread out under him, hips rolling toward his in a sensuous rhythm, hair spread out, her gaze hot and full of anticipation and pleasure as they came together again and again. Memories of her laughing with him, challenging him, filling him.

He wanted her. Just like that. Right now.

He forgot about the hard bench and pulled her closer, nearly into his lap as he let the lace of her dress pleasure his fingers.

She tilted her head, sucking him deeper, her hands sliding across his back, gripping his waist. Driving him wild with the need she'd enflamed with a simple touch. He wanted to feel her again, feel like the world was his for the taking, like life had endless possibilities. How had he not realized that Cass had been such a huge piece of that?

Masterfully, purposefully, she kissed him, breaking down everything he'd thought he was doing here. Everything went out the window: plans, strategy, formulas. Who cared? This was pleasure at its finest and he wanted more.

Then she pulled back, separating from him before he was ready, and his knees went weak. She smiled, her expression heavy with something he couldn't identify.

"Nice," she said conversationally. "And now it's time for the business talk we've been avoiding. Join me when you're done with the pleasure part of the evening."

She stood, swishing away from him on her dangerously sexy heels and sashaying out of the hall. The ice in her spine appeared firmly in place.

Blearily, he watched her go, too floored to call out. That had been hotter than he could have ever imagined. Hotter than it had ever been with Cass in the past. Hotter than he would have credited, given the ice-goddess routine she'd perfected.

He'd goaded her into kissing him in hopes of getting past all that icy reserve, past her CEO exterior, past all this business talk so he could seduce her into his bed. Instead of melting her, he'd learned he wasn't quite over Cassandra Claremont. And she hadn't been affected at all.

That turnabout was anything but fair.

Six

Gage paid the tab and followed Cass out of the restaurant.

Thank God he was behind her. That gave her a good three minutes to get her shakes under control.

It wasn't long enough. By the time they hit the sidewalk and Gage gave the valet his ticket, she'd almost managed to stop hyperventilating.

That kiss still singed her lips. His touch still burned her back. Worse? She'd touched him, too. Her own fingertips had reacquainted themselves with Gage's broad shoulders, thick hair, muscular torso. They'd explored him thoroughly and she ached to memorize him all over again.

She was supposed to be seducing him so she could get some answers about his involvement in her company's problems. Somehow that hadn't happened. She had to get the advantage back. Pronto.

As they waited in tense silence for his Hummer to appear at the curb, she prayed he wouldn't try to corner her again, maybe in one of the shadowy alcoves off to the right, where he could back her up against the brick away from prying eyes and kiss her like that again. Because she could almost feel the bite of that brick against her back. Could almost feel his hands on her. His mouth.

That would be...too much. And it was all she could think about.

"Hi, Cass. I thought that was you."

The enthusiastic female voice on her right snapped her out of the fantasy where Gage had hiked up her dress as he kissed her in that shadowy alcove and... *Get a grip, for crying out loud.*

Cass turned. And her heart tripped as she came face-to-face with Fyra's accounting manager. Who was eyeing Gage with undisguised interest as she gripped her own date's arm.

"Hi, Laurie," Cass croaked before clearing her Gage-riddled throat.

"Fancy seeing you here," Laurie commented and gestured to the man with her. "This is my husband, Mark. You may remember him from the Christmas party? But I haven't had the pleasure," she said to Gage, sticking out her hand in expectation.

Oh, no. This was not the time or place to be caught with a rival CEO. They needed to play it cool and extract themselves without—

"Gage Branson," he announced cheerily, completely ignoring the elbow Cass had just shoved in his ribs.

Too late. She stifled a groan as Laurie's expression lit up.

"Not *the* Gage Branson of GB Skin? I'm a huge fan of your body wash. I use it all the time, but don't tell my husband," she said with a laugh.

Cass glowered at her but Laurie just shrugged. "What?

Ours is too flowery. Men's scents are more outdoorsy. Lemon and sage and such."

Gage grinned. "That's what I like to hear."

The mutual admiration club gained another member when Laurie's husband jumped into the mix to announce his own GB Skin product preferences. This was beyond uncomfortable. Not simply because it grated to hear that Gage had one-upped her, but also because he'd just kissed her.

Could Laurie and Mark tell? Of course they could she was probably mussed, and she hadn't had a chance to slick on more lipstick. It was a cardinal sin to stand here on the curb with missing makeup. They'd probably noticed her naked lips the moment she'd turned around.

Okay, yes. She'd been kissing the CEO of GB Skin. Cass had kissed Gage. Strictly in the name of finding out whether he'd been the mastermind behind the leak, which had somehow turned into something else.

Her guilty conscience was probably seeping from her pores. She had to get out of here.

Cass gritted her teeth and broke in at an opportune moment. "Laurie, you know we welcome suggestions from employees on Fyra's products. Just send me an email with your thoughts about how to improve the scents in our body wash, and I'll get it into the right hands."

"Oh, I know I shouldn't be gushing over a competitor's products in front of my boss's boss." Laurie's giggle was the opposite of contrite. "But I figured it was okay to admit it. After all, I'm just using the products, not dating the CEO."

"Oh, this isn't a date," Cass interjected swiftly. "Mr. Branson is…uh—"

"Providing consulting services to Ms. Claremont," Gage finished for her smoothly. "Cass and I went to college together and she contacted me to ask for strategic advice."

"That's a pretty fancy dress for a business meeting." Laurie sighed a little over it. "I would love to be able to wear something that sexy."

Her husband murmured something in her ear and she laughed as the valet rolled up in a Lexus. "That's our ride. Nice to meet you."

The couple disappeared into the interior of the car.

"A consultant, Gage? Really?" Cass muttered as the valet parked the Hummer behind the Lexus. A horn blared behind her but she didn't take her focus off the traitor at her shoulder.

"Yeah." He opened her door and helped her into the monstrously high seat without asking. Which she appreciated because she hated needing help.

As he handed her up, she pretended she didn't notice that his fingers brushed her thigh and hung around a little longer than was absolutely necessary. Just like she was pretending she wasn't remembering what had happened a few minutes ago. But noticing was a little hard to stop once she'd opened that Pandora's box.

When he slid into his own seat, he glanced at her. "Would you have rather I corrected you? I can run up to the window of Mark and Laurie's Lexus and let them know it really *is* a date. I'm sure the company grapevine would catch fire as quickly as that news would travel."

"I get the point."

"Thank you, Gage," he mimicked in a high voice. "You're the best, Gage. Your quick thinking saved me, Gage."

A spurt of laughter burst out through her clamped lips. How dare he make her have a good time? He was not allowed to be funny and charming. And sexy. Or such a good kisser. There should be a law.

How in the world did Gage get her to have fun on this date that wasn't a date?

She sobered and crossed her arms. "It wasn't a terrible cover. Now you can come by in the morning to continue digging into the leak. The other girls know you were my mentor and they'll believe me if I say I'm consulting with you."

He shot her an amused once-over, brows raised and she resisted sinking down in the seat.

"Thank you, Gage," she said in a high voice, imitating him mimicking her because she was not about to admit she should have already thanked him. "You're the best, Gage. And so on."

She didn't like how masterfully he'd handled her. It was supposed to be the other way around.

"That's more like it." Oblivious to her sarcasm, he grinned and nodded out the windshield. "Where to?"

Everything rolled off him like water off a duck's back. She wished she had that skill; she had to work at making it *appear* as if she did, when in truth, nothing rolled off. He'd missed teaching her that back in college— how to not care about anything and always squeeze the maximum amount of fun out of everything.

Perhaps she needed to practice. Retreating wouldn't get her what she needed—answers. She threw her shoulders back.

"Turn at the next light," she instructed impulsively. "There's a great little area that overlooks the lake."

As it wasn't too far from her house, she often used the trail for jogging, though she'd never been there at night. The spot had nighttime assignation written all over it.

"Are you asking me to *park*, Ms. Claremont?" The innuendo in his tone was half amused and half *hell, yeah*.

She forced a laugh as he followed her directions and pulled into the parking lot. "I'm asking you to stroll. It's a walking path."

They could walk along the secluded moonlit path and she'd get him comfortable enough so she could ask a few pointed questions. And then when he least expected it, she'd move in for the kill.

It was no less than he deserved.

And she'd keep the reminder front and center, no matter how good it felt to be with him again. He'd kissed her. She'd kissed him back. No big deal. She didn't have to fall in love with every man she kissed. In fact, she'd never fallen in love with any man she'd kissed. Except one.

The key here was to work with Gage to find his connection to the leak and go on. A kiss was just a kiss. Emotions didn't belong in the middle of this and she'd make sure to keep it that way.

No problem.

She wished she didn't have to keep reminding herself of that.

"There's a gate with a keypad," she called over her shoulder as they slid from the car. "This part of the lake is only for residents. Follow me."

The area was secluded, with one dim light that illuminated only a small circle of the concrete lot. Trees marched away from the lot along the line of the path, sheltering it from the outside world.

"Sure." Gage's voice had deepened in the dark, skittering along her bare skin and burrowing underneath to heat up her insides, as if he'd whispered erotic instructions instead of merely agreeing with her.

Lights would be good here. Gage and the dark mixed like oil and water.

Except she didn't have any lights to turn on. The dark blanketed them both as they walked to the gate, wrapping them in a secluded bubble that felt entirely too intimate.

As she punched in the key code, Gage's presence swept along her back, igniting her nerve endings with sensuous heat. He wasn't physically touching her, but she could feel him, hear his breath. Maybe even sense the beat of his heart.

The urge to move backward, flush against his body, almost overtook her and she bit her lip. He'd be warm, solid. Her core flooded with sharp desire and she covered her gasp with a cough.

The key panel flashed red. Wrong code. Dang it.

"Problem?" Gage murmured and leaned forward, decimating the space between their bodies.

Who was she kidding? Gage and darkness went together like chocolate and peanut butter. The dark was where he did his best work, wove his best spells. Wreaked the most destruction.

"I...fat fingered it," she muttered back. "Give me a sec."

She got it right the second time. How, she'd never know.

The gate swung open on well-oiled hinges and that's when the moon blessed her with an appearance, washing the path and the lake below with a silver sheen. Perfect timing. Her nerves couldn't take much more and the dark would only tempt the devil to perform his black magic.

"There's a gazebo a few hundred yards up the path," she murmured. "We can talk."

Yes, talking. She grasped on to the concept like a lifeline, hoping the short walk would allow her to get her brain in working order again. If everything went according to plan, she'd have the solid proof she needed to implicate Gage in the leak and then she could drop him like a hot potato.

Gage, to his credit, strolled to the moonlit gazebo as instructed. The heady scent of man and sage wound through the stillness, distracting her. She never would have identified the faint herbal notes of Gage's aftershave without Laurie's comments in front of the restaurant and now it was all she could do to keep from sticking her nose in the hollow of his shoulder bone.

"So," she said as she glided up the gazebo stairs and leaned on the railing to peer out over the silvery lake. "You must have some great ears to the ground to have such detailed information about my formula."

He leaned against a post, arms crossed, and watched her as if the gorgeous panorama beyond the gazebo didn't exist. "Pardon me if I have very little interest in that subject right this minute."

She glanced at him and he wasn't even bothering to conceal his thoughts. Which must be very naughty indeed judging by the lascivious once-over he gave her. Answering heat gathered in her core, totally against her will.

All at once, she wished for a bunch of clouds to cover the moon. At least in the dark, she could pretend she didn't notice how he had such a beautiful body and gorgeous face, both of which had become more interesting with age. She shuddered as she recalled the way he'd kissed her. More heat flashed across her skin.

Why did he do that to her?

"It's a great subject," she corrected, ignoring the corkscrewing pulls inside her abdomen. "Very important. I'm just curious where you heard about it. If we're going to stop the leak, it might help to work our way backward."

"You think?" he murmured as he unwound from his

casual pose against the post to advance on her. "What if I want to talk about something else?"

She held her ground as he drew up within a hairs-breadth of touching her. "Like what?"

Without hesitation, he grabbed her hand, pulling her flush against him. Her body fell into alignment with his, nestling into the grooves like a mascara wand meeting eyelashes. His arms settled around her and somehow her head tipped back, exposing her throat to his hot perusal.

"Like how it would feel to kiss you when there's no danger of anyone interrupting us."

"Gage," she said and cursed the breathless delivery. She might as well announce how her core had gone liquid the moment his hard muscles came in contact with her curves. "Let go."

"Are you sure that's wise?" he murmured, holding her closer, which she would have sworn was impossible. "You sound a little faint. I wouldn't want you to collapse."

God, he felt good.

She needed to go on a real date, obviously, with a nice man who would treat her well and drink the wine she'd ordered. They'd have a pleasant evening ending with a romantic nightcap at her place and then he'd gently and attentively make love to her.

Above all, when she told him what to do, he'd do it.

"I'm okay. Thanks," she threw in before he started mimicking her again.

"*I'm* not okay." He bent his head to murmur into her ear. "And I like you where you are."

His breath on her skin and his hard thigh between her legs—hell, his voice alone—ripped through her in a white-hot streak of lust.

Insanity. She needed that nice man, pronto, so she could slake this thirst. A couple of rounds with Mr. Gentle-and-

Attentive and she'd be good for another year or so. Gage Branson wouldn't cause so much as a blip on her sex radar.

"This is supposed to be business only," she reminded him, but her voice cracked in the middle of the sentence and she doubted he was listening anyway.

"Hold still."

Eyes on her hair, he reached up and plucked one chopstick from her chignon, tossed it to the wooden slats under their feet and went for the other one as she yelped.

"What are you doing?" she protested as her hair spilled down her back.

"I couldn't help it." His own voice broke as he threaded both hands through the strands, winding up the locks around his fingers, a groan rumbling in his chest that vibrated her rib cage. "Your hair. It's so beautiful. Why do you put it up?"

"It's professiona—"

His mouth hit hers and stole the rest of her words as he kissed her into stunned silence. Hot and wet, his tongue slid through her lips and pleasured her relentlessly.

Tugs at her hair tilted her head back, and he took her deeper into the sensuous haze. She lost all sense of up or down, all sense period because, *oh, yes*, Gage was kissing her again and she wanted it.

The emotional tangle? Not on the agenda. If she could separate business from pleasure, she could surely separate pleasure from love. No broken hearts this time. She'd take a lesson from the King of Fun and have some.

Without warning, he pushed her against the wooden post. It wasn't brick biting into her back. Close enough.

His mouth drifted to her throat as his hands untangled from her hair to cup the back of her head, drawing her against his magic lips. She arched into him, and a moan escaped her throat, echoing in the still night.

All at once, his hands seemed to be everywhere, racing down her sides, at her shoulders. Pushing down the neckline of her dress. Her breasts sprang free of the fabric and he cupped one, bending to draw her taut nipple into his mouth.

She gasped. Exquisite. The pulls of his mouth and tongue buckled her knees but he had her. Yes, he did. He held her firmly in place as he pleasured her with his talented mouth. Shutting her eyes, she let the pleasure fork through her, damp heat gathering at her center until she thought she would burst if he didn't...

He did. One hand snaked under her dress and found her folds beneath the scrap of underwear. The barrier didn't exist to him. Clever fingers danced over her burning flesh, inside. Out.

Anyone could walk by. It heightened the pleasure... somehow. She hissed and opened wider, encouraging him to go deeper. Faster. Her breath came quicker as he drove her relentlessly, sucking at her breast, touching her intimately.

And then one final stroke shattered her resistance. She rode wave after wave of release, crying out at the strength and intensity of the pleasure he'd given her. *Gage. Smart,* funny, tender, amazing Gage. She'd missed him.

That was...not good. Oh, it had been *good*. But somehow he'd gotten below the surface, past her emotional armor.

When she floated back down from the heavens, he was watching her. He leaned in to set her dress back to rights, hands lingering, touching, pleasuring, and he murmured, "Take me back to your place. I want to do that again properly."

Again? She shook off the miasma of Gage and stared up at him, stricken with guilt. That beautiful face stared back at her and she longed to fall into him again without reservation, without fear. Without complications. Without agendas.

What was she *doing*? This wasn't the time to be playing around with fire, not with her career at stake and her company on the brink of disaster. Not when she wasn't sure she could actually stay emotionally uninvolved. She couldn't be vulnerable to him again, couldn't fathom how she'd pick herself up if he flattened her. *Could. Not.*

"I…can't."

And then her throat closed, forcing her to swallow the rest.

His expression blanked and he stepped back, releasing her. "Okay."

His tone said it was anything but. He didn't press her, though, which she was pathetically grateful for. Because if he had, he'd probably have broken down her resistance in about four seconds.

Yeah, she was a whiz at separating business and pleasure. The moment his flesh touched hers, all thoughts of business went out the window and she'd forgotten about digging for his secrets entirely.

That wasn't going to work. She had to get back in the game.

Gage dropped Cass off at her house with a terse goodnight.

They hadn't spoken at all after she shut him down. Apparently, she could flip the ice-goddess switch at will, melting in his arms for a gorgeous orgasm that nearly finished him off, as well, and then hardening her spine right back into place.

He was slipping if that hadn't gotten him an invitation into her bed. Cass had matured in many intriguing ways, but she'd also grown…distant. He had to figure out how to get rid of that space between them or he'd lose his bid for the formula. This was one competition he could not afford to lose.

When he got back to his hotel, frustrated and alone, Arwen greeted him at the door, leash in her mouth. He groaned. Last thing he needed right now. "All right."

Happily, she sniffed her way in the dark to the small park across from his hotel, zigzagging between clumps of bushes as she always did. It got a small smile from him. He hadn't been able to send her home and midnight walks in the park were due penance.

Unfortunately, Arwen didn't talk so he was left with his thoughts for company and they were anything but restful.

This thing with Cass was a problem. She was making him lose his focus on the end game. He still didn't know why she'd asked him to help her or what that silly game at dinner had been about, but one thing was for sure— he'd fully intended to find out. That was before she'd put on that cranberry dress and driven him to thorough distraction.

Of course, his solution to eliminating the distraction had been—and would continue to be—burning off their mutual, insanely hot attraction with a night of uninhibited passion. Then, with that out of the way, they both could concentrate on the business at hand: the leak.

He hoped. He couldn't deny he wanted Cass more fiercely than he could ever recall wanting a woman. Maybe more. He still ached with unfulfilled release and it was an unpleasant reminder that somewhere in the middle of all of this, getting his hands on Cass had started to eclipse getting his hands on her formula. Somehow, his plan to remind her of what she owed him had vanished and become a plan to reacquaint himself with Cass as a lover.

That was an even bigger problem. He was not going home without that formula. So far, he wasn't balancing his two agendas very well.

That changed *la mañana*.

Seven

"Hi, Melinda," he said easily to Fyra's receptionist the next morning. "I have a nine o'clock with Ms. Claremont."

"Good morning, Mr. Branson," she chirped. "She's expecting you."

Looked as though Cass had already cleared the decks for their leak discussion, which was masquerading as a "consulting" gig. The cover story had been quick thinking on his part, if he did say so himself.

He knocked on her open door. Cass was waiting for him, leaning on the front of her desk, arms crossed over a sleek pantsuit. Chopsticks peeked over the edge of her crown and dang if his fingers didn't curl at the sight of them, itching to yank them out.

He tore his gaze away. *Focus.*

"Ready to get to work?" Cass asked coolly as if last night had never happened.

"Sure." He grinned to dispel the heavy vibe and slid

into one of the chairs on the visitor's side of the desk. No power plays today. None of them had worked anyway.

Well…they'd worked to a degree. After all, he'd had Cass in his arms twice last night. That was progress. Very hot, very spectacular progress. His body sprang fully alert.

Focus, he reminded himself.

"I have a couple of thoughts I wanted to run by you," she said.

She seemed agitated, though he couldn't put his finger on what had given him that impression when she closely resembled an ice sculpture. A subtlety in her tone, maybe.

"Do any of them start with *Gage* and end with the word *naked*?"

Cass's mouth tightened. So that hadn't been the best tactic, even though he'd been kidding in an attempt to lighten the mood. Mostly. He could no sooner forget his outrageous attraction to her than he could leave without the formula. The dual agendas were supposed to complement each other, not be at war. It was killing him.

"Not in the slightest." The frost in her voice needed to go. "I've already done a couple of hours' worth of research. Now that you're here, I want to go over my notes with you."

Would she balk if he yanked her into his lap and kissed that frown upside down? Since the door was open, he resisted. But only just. And only for now.

It was better to deal with business during daylight hours. Probably.

"All right. Lay it on me. I am a fount of advice."

Her brow raised as if she didn't quite believe him. "I haven't even told you what I've got yet. How do you know you'll have anything valuable to contribute?"

"I'm motivated. Plus, you of all people should be aware of my résumé when it comes to that."

"Well, then. I'm dying to hear it, O Sage One."

Maybe her mood wasn't as volatile as he'd assumed if she was making jokes.

Memories of her, hot and pliant in his arms, damp heat against his fingers, all that hair like silk in his fingers… yeah.

It was totally worth taking a shot.

"My first piece of advice is to relax," he said smoothly. Cass hadn't moved an iota from her no-nonsense pose against the desk. Gage couldn't work his charm with her so uptight. "Second, I advise you to have dinner with me again tonight. But let's actually eat this time."

Other than a slight eye roll, she held herself impressively frozen with not even a leg tremor to give away her thoughts. "I can't display that on a presentation at a board meeting. I need results and I need them today."

"Then sit down and let's hash it out," he suggested with a nod at the other chair. "I'm starting to feel as though I was called to the principal's office the way you're towering over me."

With a piercing side eye aimed pointedly in his direction, she perched on the other chair but he had the distinct impression she didn't like the idea. He held his hands up in silent promise to keep them to himself, which she acknowledged with a muttered, "Yeah, we'll see."

The truth was he had as much of an interest in finding the leak and plugging it as Cass did—if nothing else, he wasn't prepared to hand over one single dollar until it was handled, or his investment would be worthless.

Nor could he afford to let the leak take the formula public. Then someone else might get the upper hand. The issues inside Cass's company needed to be resolved.

"Talk to me about your notes." When she hesitated, he

stuck his palms under his butt, and widened his eyes in an exaggerated *okay*? "Come on."

It was so subtle, he almost missed it. But he was watching her closely enough to pinpoint the exact moment she relaxed. The victory shot through him with a sharp thrill.

"My theory is that the leak came from someone in the lab. Has to be. No one else outside of the four founders knows how the formula works."

He'd considered that, too, and it was probably true, but she couldn't make broad assumptions. "Anyone could have hacked into your database or paid off a janitor to steal Harper's notes."

"True. But I don't think that's how it happened. So I'm thinking about planting some false information and watermarking the files. If it gets leaked, I can trace it back."

"Digital forensics? Like what banks use when they're hacked? That's expensive."

"Formula-47 is worth millions of dollars. Maybe billions."

Yes, absolutely. But you had to spend money where it made sense. "Regardless, you'd have to wait until the leak found the information and hope he or she didn't realize that the transferred files could be traced, then you have to assume the leak will decide to spill it, wait for the news to hit the industry and then try to track down who accessed the file on your server. You don't have that long."

Her lips pursed but she didn't give away anything else of her thoughts. "That's exactly why I wanted to run this by you. I knew you'd find the holes if there were any."

That small compliment from a tough customer like Cass held more weight than he would have imagined. It spread through his chest warmly. He could get used to that. Get used to combining business and pleasure in exactly this way, with a woman who could match him mentally and physically.

That's a new experience you can get behind.

Except it wasn't exactly new. This was like old times, but better because they were equals.

"It's not rocket science. I've just been around a while. Failed a lot early on and learned a few things. No big deal," he said, and he ducked his head.

She swept him with a once-over laden with—dare he hope it—some heat?

"You'll forgive me if I disagree. It's is a big deal. You're the CEO of a billion-dollar company for a reason. And I'm not. Also for a reason." Her self-deprecating shrug spoke volumes.

"Hey. You're being too hard on yourself."

Her gaze flew to his and something raw flashed in the depths, a stricken sense of anxiety. The brief spurt of emotion in her eyes sucked him in instantly, spreading through him with equal parts warmth and a desire to fix it. He almost reached out then to comfort her.

Because she needed him that way, too. And he liked being needed by a strong, independent woman like Cass.

It had nothing to do with sex, nothing to do with business—or even fun—and everything to do with why he'd recalled their relationship so fondly. Why he'd wanted to revive that between them. He liked being her go-to guy, being there for her. How had he walked away from that so easily?

Better yet, how did he keep it going now?

"Am I? How many times has one of your employees spilled company secrets?" she asked, and he didn't like how matter-of-fact she was about it.

She'd accomplished something really fantastic here at

Fyra. Insisting that a blip like the leak overshadowed that riled him up but good.

"That's not a yardstick," he insisted right back. "If it was, then you could also compare yourself to the CEOs of companies that went bankrupt or employed executives that ended up in orange jumpsuits. You're a star in comparison."

Her amused smile heated his blood unnaturally fast.

And if he could get Cass on the same page, this conversation could very well explode into something that didn't need words.

Cass let her smile widen.

She had Gage exactly where she wanted him. It had taken her a bit to shift the mood and even longer to convince Gage his charm was working on her. At this point, he was so busy flirting and shooting her heated glances, he was scarcely paying attention to the matter at hand— the leak. Advantage Cassandra.

Keeping it was another story.

"You really think so?" She leaned into him, letting her arm casually brush Gage's. His gaze darkened. "That means a lot to me."

"This is not the conversation I thought we were going to have." He shifted closer, crowding into her space and she almost flinched as the contact sang through her but caught herself in time.

That episode last night, up against the gazebo post, had kept her tossing and turning all night long. She couldn't forget it. She might never be able to jog by that gazebo again without reliving the feel of Gage's mouth on her flesh and the intensity of his heated gaze on her bare breasts as he watched her climax under his talented fingers.

It was enough to make her want to corner him, strip

him naked and let the passion between them come to conclusion. Where she got to watch *him* fall apart at *her* hands.

Which she totally planned to do…while extracting the information she needed. She could not, under any circumstances, let him dissolve that goal like he'd done last night. No more would she let her emotions run away with her. It was all business, all the time, especially while she was seducing him.

This was her career at stake, and the careers of her friends, poised to vanish into thin air if she didn't produce the name of the person responsible for disclosing company secrets.

Fyra was her life and no man could replace it. Especially not this one.

"This conversation is better," she said with a tiny smile guaranteed to pique his interest. "For example, I was just about to take your advice and ask you to dinner tonight. At my place."

That got his attention. He sat up so fast, his back teeth clacked together. "Don't toy with me, woman."

Oh, but he was so fun to toy with, especially as she gave him a taste of his own medicine.

"Does that mean you don't want to come?" she purred. "Or do you want me to tack the dinner discussion to the end of today's agenda?"

"Now I'm dying to know what topics we have to get through to reach that particular item."

"Business," she said firmly. "Then pleasure."

His hazel eyes lit up and a wicked smile spread across his face. "Just so you know, the fact that you label dinner at your place as pleasure warms my heart tremendously."

She held off the shiver because he didn't need to know he'd affected her *that* way. He *shouldn't* be affecting her that way. Her armor—the shield she easily employed with other men—seemed to soften far too easily when he was around.

"Business," she repeated. "We have to make more progress on the leak. The news broke on Monday. It's Thursday morning. I'm no closer to plugging the blabbermouth than I was then."

She'd done a considerable amount of digging this morning on her own and had found a couple of promising leads. Right before Gage had arrived, she'd ordered the most high-level background check money could buy on every last employee in this company. But he didn't have to know that. In reality, she didn't want him anywhere near her files or embroiled in a real discussion about her strategy.

His job was to tell her what his connection was to the leak. What strings he was pulling. Which angles he was playing. She needed to uncover every last secret, especially when he looked at her like he was right now, like he wanted to finish what he'd started last night in the gazebo.

Because as soon as she handed him over to the authorities, then she could remind herself with cold hard facts that he was the spawn of Satan. Somehow she kept forgetting that.

"It's a problem," he agreed far too easily.

Suspicious of his capitulation, she nodded. "Right. We find the leak and then we can think about pursuing a… personal relationship."

She caressed the term with her voice as suggestively as she could. She had to regain the upper hand.

"Oh, no, sweetheart," he growled. "You have it all backward. That orgasm last night? Only the beginning of what's in store for you. For both of us. It's an absolute necessity that we start there and then worry about the leak."

His heavy, masculine vibe snaked through the room,

engulfing her. Tempting her down the wrong path, where she craved that pleasure, that connection more than anything else. "That makes no sense."

His intense gaze zeroed in on her and she felt it deep inside, where he'd thoroughly woken up her latent sex drive. He didn't move, didn't touch her, and somehow that was more powerful than if he had.

"It's the only thing that makes sense. We're not going to get anything accomplished until this fire between us is extinguished. Admit it. You know it's true."

She hated to say it…but he might have a point. Worse, she couldn't think of one solid argument against it, but she had to try as a matter of principle. "That's your logic? We're not disciplined enough to work together so we should just screw around instead?"

He didn't flinch. "If you want logic, then do it for the best reason of all. You want to. And I want you, Cassandra."

His deep voice caressed her name, unleashing another wave of desire that grew very hard to contain. This was a seduction, plain and simple, but she'd lost track of who was seducing whom. Besides, dragging it out wouldn't change things. It was just sex. She wasn't going to fall for him again. Why deny herself what she wanted?

Maybe she'd failed thus far to get him to admit anything incriminating because she really needed to get him naked first. Naked and sated.

"I dug up some paper archives from Harper's research over the past few years that have names of the employees attached to each stage of the development. Can we at least pretend to do some work tonight?" she asked as the compelling force of his smile nearly drew her into his space, magnetically, like she'd transformed into a pile of metal pins straining toward him.

"Sure. If that's what turns you on, I'm game."

"Be at my place at seven." Her turf, her rules. And there was no way she'd let him get to her like he'd done last night. Ruthless detachment was the only way. "I'll bring the files and you bring the drinks since you're such a big baby about wine. I have until tomorrow to report progress back to the other executives. So we definitely have to do *some* work."

Hopefully she'd discover she did her best work between the sheets.

He grinned and saluted. "Wear something sexy and I'll read every one of those files word for word."

She'd removed all the proprietary information from the files and her employee's names were posted on the company website, so she had no qualms about sharing that information with him. With enough incentive, he might slip up and clue her in that he recognized one of the names. "It's a deal."

She just had to be very careful to ensure the only slipping going on was on his side.

Eight

Later that night, Gage picked up a bottle of cachaça, some limes and a bag of brown sugar, just in case Cass didn't have any on hand. Caipirinhas were a far sight more tolerable than margaritas, and women usually loved the way he made them. Plus the drink was about 85 percent alcohol, which gave a nice buzz but, because cachaça was distilled from sugarcane, the next morning didn't come with a busting headache.

On his way to Cass's house, Gage dropped Arwen off at a doggie daycare. With that heartbreaking task out of the way, he drove to Cass's house. She was worth a furious vizsla and the probability of an additional fee upon pickup after Arwen drove everyone at the daycare to the brink of insanity.

Cass opened the door, barefoot and clad in shorts that showed a mile of leg, thank the good Lord, and a fitted T-shirt that most women couldn't have done justice. On

Cass, it was legendary. She'd twisted her hair up in a messy waterfall of a hairdo that was somehow more suggestive than the chopsticks.

His mouth went dry.

"Hey," she said, opening the door wider, which lifted the hem of her T-shirt just a flash, revealing a slice of bare stomach. "Hope casual is okay. I thought low-key might help us get some work accomplished tonight."

Yeah, no. She needed a better mirror if she thought that what she had on was supposed to provide some kind of Gage repellant. Her toes were hot pink, for crying out loud, which drew his attention to her bare feet again and again.

"Oh, good," he said when he could speak. "I was worried I wouldn't be able to keep my hands off you. *Whew.*"

He mimed wiping his brow in relief and she shot him a sunny smile that heightened the flame inside his gut.

She motioned him inside and called over her shoulder. "Should we start on the paperwork first, then? Maybe later we can have a drink and relax."

Seriously?

"That was sarcasm," he said bluntly as he blew over the threshold, shutting the door behind him with a loud bang.

She whirled, clearly startled by the sudden noise, and smacked into his chest. Right where he wanted her. He set down his bag of goodies—caipirinhas had totally lost his interest.

"If you wanted me to keep my hands off you," he growled, hauling her into his arms. "A better plan would have been to move to Timbuktu."

He hustled her backward, against the wall, and shoved a thigh between her legs. Hard and high. She gasped, a throaty sound that crawled inside him and lit the fuse of a row of fireworks residing in his groin, threatening to explode without notice.

"In case you're not clear on this," he continued, nipping at her ear as he leaned in. The full body contact sang through him. "I want you. *Now.* Not later."

Her nipples pebbled against his chest as he rolled his hips to fit more snuggly against hers. Those shorts were made of much thinner fabric than he'd guessed and her heat engulfed his steel-hard lower half. Lust licked through his blood like a wildfire.

He needed her hot and pliant immediately, before he lost it. There was no way she would get the opportunity to leave him hanging like she had last night. Oh, he'd enjoyed every second of making her come against that post, moonlight spilling over her gorgeous body, while they were both fully dressed. It had ranked as one of the hottest experiences of his life. But tonight he deserved a turn, too.

He ached to reacquaint himself with her body, the way she tasted, the way she would respond to his touch. That T-shirt, soft under his fingers, promised delights underneath it and he was game to discover them.

No one was around and they had all night. He planned to make the most of it.

They gazed at each other and the ocean of desire in her eyes twisted through him. She was inside him already and he welcomed her with a sense of awe. How had she made him feel this way before they'd scarcely gotten started?

"I want you," he repeated hoarsely, but the phrase scarcely encompassed the sheer need he was trying to describe, as if he depended on her for his next breath. "And not because you're wearing a sexy outfit. Because you have a brain. Because you challenge me. Because I like being around you. Because—"

"If you're going to kiss me, shut up and do it."

"That might be the sexiest thing you've ever said."

Because it suited him, he tilted her head back and took her mouth with his, open and wet, pleasing them both with the force of his tongue. She tasted of fire and woman and he wanted more. So he went deeper, coaxing her to meet him with increased passion. No holding back. No ice goddess, not tonight.

Apparently of the same mind, she moaned and shifted against his thigh, her fingers working at his waistband. She pulled his shirt free and spread her palms across his back. Oh, yeah. *Heaven.* He'd captured his very own angel. Her touch raced down his spine and dipped into his pants, resting on his butt. She shoved, grinding his erection against her.

Nothing angelic about that.

Sensation exploded. In his body. In his head. She was taking over, taking her own pleasure, and he was hard-pressed to find an argument against it. Bolder now, she rubbed against his shaft, nearly finishing him off. He clawed back the release through will alone.

With her barriers down, she was hotter than he'd imagined. Duly noted.

With a groan, he fumbled with the hem of her shirt and finally, his fingers closed around it. Gone. Next? Bra. Also gone.

Her gorgeous breasts fell into his palms, heavy and hot. She was made for him, filling his hands perfectly. Locking his lips onto one erect nipple, he swirled his tongue around it as he worked the rest of her clothes into a heap, desperate to have her flesh against his. His pulse beat in his throat as she stripped him in kind, then urged him on with her hands against his thighs.

"Wait, darling," he murmured, and in moments, he'd sheathed himself with a condom.

Boosting her up against the wall, he slid into her heat and pinned her in place, reveling in the perfection of her tightness. *Yes.* Exactly where he belonged. Inside her.

She wrapped her legs around him and thrust her hips, drawing him deeper. And deeper still. She gasped out tiny moans of pleasure that drove him wild.

He needed to touch her…but he couldn't let go or she'd fall. From this angle, the sensation was unbelievable. Then she widened her hips, changing the pressure and his moans mingled with hers.

This wasn't the Cass he recalled. This woman was on fire, taking what she wanted, giving unconditionally. Finding his pleasure center easily and drawing him higher and higher, against his will. He'd planned to savor. To reclaim.

But this Cass, who was every inch his equal, was claiming him, wholly.

He couldn't hold back one second longer, but somehow managed to get a thumb between their bodies, stimulating her the way she'd always preferred and that set her off. At last. The ripples of her climax closed around him a moment before his answering climax exploded.

Sweet, blessed release. He shut his eyes and drove home one last time, drawing out the pleasure for them both. When he could feel his legs again, he swung her around and slid to the ground, still holding her in his lap. He tilted his head against hers, both of them breathless, chests heaving from exertion.

That had been…something else. Nothing like it had been before. It had been hot and erotic and the stuff of X-rated fantasies. She'd always been amazing but they'd never gotten so caught up that they couldn't make it to the bed. They were still in her foyer. He'd meant to be gentler, less frenzied. He'd envisioned a slow, sweet reintroduction to each other, but who could complain about a fast, unbelievably intense reintroduction?

Thankfully, they'd gotten that out of their systems.

"Maybe now we can concentrate," he muttered. But he didn't think so.

Cass ended up ordering pizza from the place around the corner. After the hallway gymnastics, her bones had melted away entirely and she couldn't stand long enough to cook. Gage had been amazing. Strong, tender, hot, sweet. Far more so than she'd expected or remembered.

True to his word, he got down to business and they read files while drinking a pitcher of the limey, sugary concoction he'd put together. It was delicious. But not as delicious as Gage. Or the conversation they fell into as they were reading. It was like old times—and her insides, which were not all that solid in the first place, mushed under the dual onslaught of sexy man and alcohol.

Names. She needed to focus on these names. She steeled her spine, hardened her heart and ignored all the sizzling sidelong glances he shot her way.

This was about sex and work. Only. After all, he'd practically dared her to prove she could separate business and pleasure. No emotions necessary for that.

She had Gage read the names out loud and as he did, she offered her impression of the person, their work ethic, any workplace drama she knew of. As she talked, she watched Gage carefully for any flicker of recognition. Nothing. Either he was very good at keeping his cards close to the vest or the leak's name wasn't on this list.

Of course, deep inside she recognized the possibility that he wasn't involved. The longer they spent in each other's company, the more she'd started to hope that he wasn't. Because if his interest in the formula was innocent, then it changed everything between them.

And she wanted that. Oh, how she wanted things to be different, with the possibility of throwing their agendas out the window and just connecting as man and woman.

It was madness. Gage could not be trusted under any circumstances and obviously sex had only confused things, not clarified them. She kicked him out before she started imagining things that were impossible, like asking him to stay and hold her all night.

He left without arguing, which dug under her skin and sat there irritating her for no apparent reason. Why? He'd done what she asked—what more could she want? Gage did not belong in her bed. That was reserved for men who wanted to stick around and he wasn't the type. A few days and then *gone*.

She knew that. But that didn't stop all the needy dreams during the long night where he curled around her in bed and stroked her hair and told her everything was going to be okay, that he was here for her and she didn't have to be strong with him. That he understood her and cared about her.

Clearly a dream—Gage Branson wasn't marriage material and she didn't need a man who whispered pretty lies in her ear about the state of things. There was no guarantee even one blessed thing in her life would turn out okay. The investigative work she'd done on her own time hadn't amounted to much and Gage hadn't given up any information either, which meant she was still at square one.

Around 5:00 a.m. she crawled from the big, lonely bed and tried to rinse Gage off her body and soul with a hot shower. It was Friday. Reckoning day. Trinity had scheduled a meeting with the four executives to hear Cass's progress report on the leak. It was shaping up to be a short meeting because she had nothing to report.

It took twice as long as normal to do her makeup, partly due to her shaking hands and partly due to the necessity of taking extra care to present her best "I've got this" face to the world. Then, she dressed carefully in a black suit with a knee-length skirt and red silk shell. The look radiated power and control and she needed both today.

By nine, the other ladies filed in to take their customary seats around the conference table. Cass had been in her chair for fifteen minutes, going over nonexistent notes, and calming her nerves. It should have been the other way around. Lots of progress, cool as a cucumber.

There was a distinct possibility she might throw up.

New fine lines around Harper's eyes spoke to the heightened level of stress on Fyra's chief science officer. She'd been clocking long hours in anticipation of presenting Formula-47 for FDA approval, perhaps in vain if Cass didn't get with the program. Trinity tapped one foot, impatient and ready to draw blood the moment someone presented their jugular. *Someone* was about to be Cass, she had a feeling. Eyes on her legal pad, Alex wore a slight frown, as if this boardroom was the last place she wanted to be and Cass had interrupted the CFO's more important agenda items for the day.

"Thanks for taking time from your busy Friday to hear my progress report," Cass began smoothly and squared her tablet, trying to get her emotions under control. She'd failed to do her job and her partners needed to know it, no matter how hard it was to admit she didn't have it all together.

If only she'd gotten some sleep last night, her emotions wouldn't be riding so close to the surface. If only she'd checked her mushy heart at the door when Gage came over, she could have gone all night with him and maybe extracted something useful. Instead, she'd kicked him out because she couldn't control anything, let alone herself.

"I'll cut to the chase," Cass said and met the gaze of each of her partners in turn. "I haven't found anything yet."

The three women's expressions ranged from disbelief to anger.

Alex spoke first. "What do you mean, you haven't found anything yet? You've had all week." She sank down in her chair an inch, as if Cass's news had physically added weight to her shoulders, which increased the general despair in the room. "This is awful. We should have involved the authorities from the beginning."

"We couldn't have," Cass reminded her. She cleared the catch from her throat. They'd had this discussion on Monday when the trade magazine had hit the industry and again on Tuesday in their board meeting. "Mike said the article was too vague, remember? We don't have any recourse but to investigate ourselves."

"Which has failed miserably." Alex crossed her arms and stared at Cass. "We trusted you with this. We could have all been working on it but you said you'd handle it. What, exactly, did you do all week?"

Cass took the harsh question without flinching. "I have a list of suspects. Everyone who's had their hands on Formula-47 over the past two years and could reasonably understand how it works."

The betrayer's name was on that list—she knew it like she knew her own face. How else would Gage's additional information about Fyra's yet-to-be-released product offering be so accurate? It was the only explanation. Now she just had to find a way to prove it. And convince the others to give her more time.

Trinity's chair squeaked as she swiveled it toward Cass. "So the article is too vague to involve the authorities, but when your old boyfriend shows up with more detailed information, that's not enough to go to the cops?"

Heat flushed through Cass's cheeks. Blushing? Really? She never did that. Thankfully, Harper's color-correcting foundation should hide the worst of it. "I'm working that angle. In case he's involved."

"Oh." Light dawned in Trinity's expression. "I thought that whole consulting thing was weird. I was convinced Gage was hanging around in hopes of swooping in for another chance to break your heart. It never occurred to me that you were the one working him. Good for you."

Alex's brows snapped together. "What, like you're sleeping with him to find out if he coordinated the leak? That's horrible."

A squeak of denial almost escaped Cass's clamped lips.

But she couldn't deny it. That was exactly what she was doing, but hearing it from Alex did make it sound horrible. Something sad crawled through her chest and she couldn't breathe.

Why? They were just fooling around anyway. Nothing serious was going on, so it wasn't as if he was going to get *his* heart broken. She wasn't even sure he had one to break.

And *how* in God's name had her friends figured out so quickly that she and Gage weren't strictly business associates this time around? Somehow this whole conversation had become a cross-examination of Cass's sex life.

"It's brilliant," Trinity insisted. "Men do stuff like that all the time and no one thinks anything of it. About time we turn the tables. Screw him and then screw him over, Cass."

Finally Trinity was defending her, and if only she hadn't been so enthusiastic about Cass's new status as a ballbreaker, it might have made Alex's accusations more tolerable.

"It's true," Cass admitted. "I'm keeping my eye on him from close quarters just in case he lets something incriminating slip."

"Was that before or after he seduced away your good sense?" Alex asked derisively. "You'll forgive me if I find your investigative techniques suspect. No one can fully separate business from sex. It's impossible."

Not for me.

Cass started to say it out loud, to defend herself against Alex's blatant charge that she'd compromised Fyra due to her personal relationship with Gage, such as it was. She should tell them unequivocally that she wouldn't allow a naked man to distract her from what she knew she needed to do.

But she couldn't say it. What if Gage *was* involved in the leak and she missed it because she was too busy day-dreaming about him magically transforming into some-one she could count on? That very possibility was exactly the reason the board meeting had descended into girl talk about the man Cass was boinking—because everyone thought she might be compromised.

Ridiculous. She was compartmentalizing just fine. The person responsible for the leak was keeping a low profile, that was all. If Gage knew anything about it, he'd trip up before long.

"Give me a few more days," she pleaded. "I know what I'm doing."

Throwing her pen down on her pad with considerable force, Alex shook her head. "No. We don't have a few more days."

Heart in her throat, Cass evaluated the other two girls,

who glanced at each other. Trinity shrugged. "I'm game for it. I kind of want to see what happens with lover boy."

Harper narrowed her gaze and flipped her ponytail over her shoulder. "Gage Branson treated you like dog food in college, Cass. While he's lighting your fire, don't fool yourself into thinking he's changed."

Red stained Harper's cheeks, likely as a result of holding back her legendary hot temper, which Cass appreciated. Alex's hostility was heartbreaking enough without adding another longtime friend to the other side of the fence.

"I've got that under control, too," Cass assured them, ignoring that sad ping inside that had only gotten worse the longer the conversation went on.

Of course Gage hadn't changed. Fortunately, Cass's eyes were wide open and soon she'd be watching him disappear down the highway. It was a fact, and wishing things could be different didn't mean she was fooling herself.

Alex's sigh was long-suffering. "This is a mistake. Have all of you forgotten that Gage runs a company that eats into our profits every stinking quarter? He's our competition, just as much as Lancôme and MAC."

And that was the bottom line in all of this. How fitting that Fyra's CFO would be the one to point that out. In marked contrast to the last time they'd been in this room, Alex's contrariness and lack of confidence had roots in reality, and that sobered Cass faster than anything else could have.

"No one's forgotten that, least of all me," Cass countered quietly. "Why do you think I'm cozying up to him? Give me a few more days."

"Fine," Alex conceded wearily. "I don't see how you're going to prove Gage is involved in the leak while he's got his tongue in your mouth, but whatever. We don't have a lot of choices."

As victories went, it felt hollow. With the leak still undetected, the company could come down like a house of cards. She got that. But it twisted her stomach to have her strategy so cold-bloodedly laid out for her. Yes, she'd planned to keep Gage close for exactly the reasons they'd discussed, but all at once, the idea didn't sit well. Gage had been…fun thus far. Almost like a friend. A confidante. Everything a lover should be. What if he *wasn't* involved?

She liked it better when her partners had been in the dark about her covert plans.

Abnormally quiet, they left the boardroom, and miraculously Cass made it all the way to her office before the shakes started. Nothing helped calm her nerves—coffee, water, a brisk walk at lunch. She had to get it together, had to find a way to produce results.

If Gage was involved in the leak, she had to figure out a way to prove it. To prove she could compartmentalize and that he wasn't affecting her ability to do her job, once and for all. She buckled down and pored over files and personnel records until she thought her eyes would bleed.

Around three o'clock, her phone vibrated and Gage's name flashed on the screen. She read the text message.

I'm in the parking lot. Ditch work and play hooky with me.

For God knew what reason, that put a smile on her face. That sounded like the perfect short-term solution to her problems.

Nine

The dark green Hummer sat in the same parking spot as it had the first time Gage had visited Fyra, under a large oak tree saved when the developers poured the concrete for Fyra's new building.

Shade nearly obscured the monstrosity of a vehicle, but Cass found it easily. With a heightened sense of anticipation, she dashed across the parking lot in hopes of hopping into the Hummer before anyone saw her.

After the unproductive day she'd had, the last thing she should be doing was leaving work at three o'clock. In her current mood, it was the only thing she could have done. Besides, this was exactly where she was supposed to be. She'd promised the others she'd make progress with Gage and the leak. No one had to know she was happy to see him.

Hooky. It used to be one of their favorite code words and it still had the same punch. Maybe more because she was skipping out on the enormous pressure inside the walls of her company instead of a boring lecture in a drafty hall. A little thrill shot through her as she clambered up into the passenger seat of Gage's car.

God, this sucked. She'd rather pretend they didn't have any more complications between them apart from where to go so they could spend an illicit couple of hours together. Strictly in the name of sex, of course. Instead, she'd spend their time together with both eyes wide open for any signs of his involvement in her company's troubles.

"Hey," Gage said, flashing her a mischievous smile. "I thought I was in for at least a couple of rounds of sexy text messages designed to get you out of your purple cave. Silly me. If I'd have known all it was going to take was one, I'd have been by at lunchtime."

"It's Friday." She waved it off as if she left early on Friday all the time, which was a flat-out lie. "I needed the break."

Especially if the break involved the man she should be sticking to like Velcro—and not because he was lickable. Which he was.

Concern filled his gaze as he pulled out of the Fyra lot. "Rough day?"

God, she was slipping. How had he realized that instantly? Gage shouldn't be the one person who saw through her, the only person who looked at her long enough to see her internal struggles.

She started to deny it but couldn't. What would be the point? "Yeah."

He drove in silence for a few minutes, but veered off the road after only a couple of miles. The Hummer rolled to a stop under the shade of a large oak tree near a deserted park.

"Come here," he commanded as he pulled her into his arms easily despite the gearshift and steering wheel.

She should have struggled more. Should have pushed him away. Sex only, nothing more. That's why she was here—for a much-needed release at the hands of a man very capable of delivering it.

But his soothing touch bled through her and nothing else could penetrate the little bubble surrounding her and Gage as he held her. *Nothing*, not the various parts of the car, not all the weight of Fyra's troubles, not the difficult past between them.

Everything faded under his tender strokes against her skin. She'd needed this, needed him. Needed someone to be there to catch her when she fell, to be on her side. His shirt was soft against her cheek and his woodsy scent filled her head, spreading the oddest sense of peace through her chest.

A tickle in her hair alerted her to the presence of his fingers a moment before both chopsticks slid free, releasing the tight chignon. Her scalp nearly cried in relief as her hair billowed down her back. He gathered the strands in his strong hands, winding them around his palms. Threading them through to his knuckles. Caressing her back.

It was relaxing and stimulating at the same time. How was that possible? But with the binding hairstyle gone, a weight lifted, almost as if he'd studied her and pinpointed precisely what she'd needed.

A groan rumbled in Gage's chest, vibrating her own, and in a snap, the atmosphere shifted. Awareness spread across her skin, sensitizing it. Switching cheeks, she rested her head in the hollow of his shoulder, but oh look, there was Gage's ear just a millimeter from her lips.

Grazing it lightly, she inhaled him, letting his powerful masculinity wash through her. The slow tide picked up speed, flowing like lava toward her toes, heating her in its wake.

Riding the flood, she arched her back, pushing her aching breasts against his chest, seeking more of his touch. She nipped at his throat, slowly working her way back to the tender lobe. When her teeth closed around it, he exhaled hard. It was ragged and thrilling, filling her with bold desire.

She licked him and oh, yes, he tasted amazing. *More.* And then his mouth was on hers and she drank from him, drawing out even more of that essence she craved. Hot and masterful, he kissed her back, meeting her tongue thrusts with his own, changing the angles to go deeper, and she moaned under the onslaught of sensation and Gage and everything she'd been missing for so long.

"Cass," he murmured against her mouth. "Let me take you to my hotel. It's five minutes away."

Five whole minutes? Too long. She didn't bother to respond and pulled him half into her seat as she went on a survey of that wicked, gorgeous body.

He sucked in a breath as she dipped into his pants and found the heated length of flesh she craved. So hard and thick and she wanted it. "Now, Gage. Don't make me wait."

With a curse, he pushed her hands off his body and moved from behind the steering wheel to slide into her seat, shoving her against the door. He promptly picked her up and resettled her on his lap, facing him, and watched her with a hooded, wicked glint to those hazel eyes as he pushed his palms against the hem of her skirt. The fabric gathered under his hands, riding up to her waist where he grabbed on and fitted their hips together, aligning his hard shaft against her center.

Perfect. Almost. Not enough. She rolled her hips, grind-

ing against him and the answering shadow of lust shooting
through his gaze heightened her own pleasure.

Without another word, he cupped her head with both
hands and pulled her against his mouth, ravishing her
with a long, wet kiss. Frantically, blindly, she worked at
his pants until he sprang free into her eager hands. Her
very own velvet-wrapped present. With her first stroke,
his head fell back against the seat, flopping his too-long
hair against his forehead and he groaned, eyes tightly shut.

That was…inspiring. She did it again, awed that she
could command the body of such a powerful man.

"Back pocket," he rasped. "Hurry."

She wasted no time rolling on the condom. Pushing up
on her thighs, she guided him to her entrance and plunged
until they joined fully in one swift rush. They moaned
in tandem as he flung his arms around her to hold her in
place, rocking her so sensuously, so soul deep, she felt
tears pricking at her eyelids. He filled her body, filled her
head, filled every millimeter of *her*.

"So good." His breath fluttered in her ear as he read
her mind. "Open for me."

To demonstrate, he widened her hips, nestling himself
even closer to her.

Slowly, more slowly than she'd thought possible for a
man on a mission, he drew her mouth to his and laid his
lips against it. Savoring. He explored her as if they had all
the time in the world, and as if she wasn't about to scream,
and just as she thought she'd come out of her skin if he
didn't move, he thrust his hips, driving deeper inside her.

She gasped and the rush overwhelmed her, pounding
in her chest, at her center. Her vision darkened as he slid
home again and again, and then his thumb found the true
center of her pleasure, swirling against it with exactly the
right pressure to set her off like a lit stick of dynamite.

The release rolled through her thickly, gathering power as she exploded over and over. She slumped against his chest as he cried out her name hoarsely, tensing through his own climax.

He held her gently, wrapped tight in his arms as if he never planned to let go. She sank down into the ocean of Gage. He surrounded her and she couldn't kick her way to the surface. Didn't want to. This was sheer bliss and it wasn't just due to the sex.

It was Gage. Only him.

"That was amazing," he murmured into her hair. "Now can we go to my hotel?"

"No." She snuggled deeper into his embrace, her nose against his neck where it smelled the most like well-loved man. "Take me home. And stay."

A mistake. He'd cracked open something inside her that should have been sealed shut.

Except she was so tired of pretending she didn't feel anything. So tired of bottling up her emotions and trying to prove she had it all together when in fact, she didn't.

Gage didn't care. He was leaving soon anyway, so why keep up pretenses? It was kind of freeing, knowing how it would end. She didn't have to worry about him breaking her heart because she wasn't going to give it to him. He didn't have to know she harbored all these feelings for him.

"That sounds like an idea I can get behind," he growled. "Or on top of, in front of, against the wall, in the shower. All of the above."

Too late to take it back now. And besides, she should have had the presence of mind to invite him deliberately. Because what better way to keep tabs on him than if they were together around the clock? That's where her mind *should* have been at.

"Stay the weekend. I know you have to go back to Austin Sunday night but until then? We'll order lots of takeout and never get dressed."

"That's a deal, Ms. Claremont."

His slow, sexy smile felt like a reward and she planned to grab her spoils with both hands. She'd spend the weekend enjoying herself and, as a bonus, she'd make solid progress on investigating Gage's involvement in the leak, just like she'd promised her partners. With the man in question in her bed, surely she could sneak a glance through his phone or keep an ear out in case he talked in his sleep. It was the best of both worlds and she didn't even have to feel guilty about it because she was looking out for Fyra first and foremost.

The other stuff—the emotional knot—wasn't a factor. She wouldn't let it be. She had to buckle on her armor a bit tighter while around Gage, that was all.

Gage untangled their clothes, hair and bodies, helping her resituate everything and then climbed back into the driver's seat. Fortunately, the park was still deserted or that would have been a helluva show.

She had one short weekend to get results on her quest for a name…before the other girls made a motion to relieve her of her position as head of the company she'd helped build from nothing.

Gage stopped by the hotel to pick up Arwen and his luggage, then checked out while Cass waited for him outside.

When he got back to the Hummer, he opened the back to stow his bags and waved for Arwen to hop in. That's when he realized this was not going to go well. She sat on her haunches and stared at the sky, the ground, a bug flying by. It was her way of saying she wasn't riding in the back like chattel.

"Don't be ridiculous," he growled. "There's a human in the front seat. You're a dog. Ride in the back. That's what they make this part of the vehicle for."

Nothing. He shook his head. They both knew she wasn't just a *dog* and this was one of the worst times in recent memory for her to remind him of it. He treated her like she was human, and she lapped it up as her due in true lady-of-the-manor style. Just because Gage had a real human to spend time with for a change didn't alter the fact that he'd spoiled her rotten due to his own lack of companionship over the years.

"What's going on?" Cass asked, her hair still loose and delicious around her shoulders.

The sight of her in that passenger seat, where she'd so sweetly offered him a fantasy weekend four seconds after giving him what he'd already thought was the ultimate encounter—amazing. He couldn't wait to dive in again.

"Arwen. In the car. Now," he muttered. "I've got a date with a shower and a wet woman and you are not going to mess it up." Louder, he called, "Just having a discussion about the proper place for a dog. One sec."

Extra motivation must have done the trick because he manhandled Arwen into the back on the first try and shut the hatch before she could leap out, which he wouldn't put past her. She gave a mournful cry that he heard even with all of the doors closed.

When he climbed into the driver's seat, Arwen had already weaseled in between the front seats, paws on the gearshift. She stuck her nose in Cass's face, clearly bent on discovering all the secrets of the woman who had usurped her spot.

Uh-oh. Arwen had never deigned to check out a woman

Gage had brought into her world. Usually she ignored them. Of course, Gage always introduced her to someone off Arwen's turf and it was rare that Arwen saw the same woman twice. Gage couldn't even remember the last time he'd had a woman in the Hummer, let alone at the same time as the vizsla.

"She's so sweet," Cass exclaimed as she rubbed Arwen's ginger head enthusiastically, earning a smile from the dog.

Gage eyed Arwen suspiciously and with no small amount of shock. She never approved of anyone female, let alone someone she'd already singled out as a rival. "Yeah, that's one word for her."

Arwen muscled her way into the front seat, right onto Cass's lap before Gage could grab her collar or even warn Cass that forty pounds of dog was coming her way.

Great. It wasn't as if Cass was wearing a fifteen-hundred-dollar suit or anything—not that he'd shown much more care when he'd crumpled it up around her waist. But still. There was a place for Arwen and it wasn't on top of Gage's...date. Former lover. Current lover. Partner in crime. Whatever.

"Sorry," he threw out. "Arwen, get in the back!"

"It's okay." Cass shot him a smile as she rearranged Arwen's paws off her bare legs. "I don't mind. It's not that far to my house and she's used to riding in the front, I would imagine."

"She is. Doesn't mean she should get her way." He started the car with one last warning glare at the dog who was predictably ignoring him. "I can drop her off at a pet hotel on the way."

Both woman and dog shook their heads.

"That's not necessary," Cass said, patting Arwen's back. "She's welcome in my backyard. I have some sad little hydrangeas that would probably benefit from being eaten."

"Really?" This time, he eyed Cass suspiciously. "She'll dig up your grass. I'm not kidding."

"So? She's been cooped up in a hotel all week, hasn't she? My yard overlooks the lake and there are always lots of birds. No reason why she can't have a nice weekend, too, is there?"

Arwen's ears perked up at the mention of birds and that seemed to decide it. Casually, as if it had been her idea all along, the dog picked her way to her own seat and lay down on it without bothering to glance at Gage.

A little dumbfounded, he drove toward Cass's house and wondered what had just happened. "Okay. Thanks. Apparently that plan got the thumbs-up from Her Royal Highness."

And from Gage. He snuck a sidelong peek at Cass. There'd always been something special about Cass but he hadn't realized her skills included dog whispering.

Warmth spread through his chest. Did Cass have any clue how much he appreciated her good humor over his bad-mannered dog? The invitation to let Arwen skip the dog hotel had earned *mucho* points with both man and beast. And neither of them gave points easily.

Arwen heartily approved of Cass's massive backyard. The moment Cass set down the bowl of water, Gage's diva of a dog gave Cass an extra nose to the hand, which was the equivalent of a rare thank-you. Would wonders never cease?

Gage followed Cass into the house, mystified why she'd be so welcoming of his dog. And why his dog was so welcoming of the woman.

Cass needs a big, fat thank-you. Immediately.

"Show me to your shower," he commanded, his body already hardening in anticipation of a hot and wet Cass.

She raised a brow. "That's the first thing you want to do? Take a shower?"

"You say that as though I'll be by myself."

"In that case…" She pivoted on one stiletto, then climbed the wide hardwood planked staircase at a brisk trot.

He raced after her, effortlessly taking the stairs two at a time, laughing as she ducked into a room and then popped back out as if to make sure he was following her. As if he'd be foolish enough to lose her.

"You're not getting away that easily," he promised as he entered what was clearly her bedroom. He made short work of whirling her into his arms so he could strip her slowly for a much-needed round two.

When her gaze met his, it was full of promise and his breath hitched in his chest as he drew off her suit one luscious piece at a time. Never one to hold back, she got him out of his clothes lickety-split and when they were both bared to each other, he picked her up and carried her into the en suite bathroom he'd spied earlier.

She flung her arms around his neck, her own breath coming faster as she nuzzled his ear. Heat swept across his skin. Would he ever get tired of her? Usually he was done by now. Once, maybe twice, was generally enough with one woman.

Not this one. She kept drawing him back and he kept not resisting.

Gently, he set down the armful of long-legged blonde on the black granite vanity so he could turn on the water in the shower. Six showerheads spurted to life and he let them run in the cavernous enclosure that had the perfect seat for what he had in mind.

Cass perched on the counter, blinking at him dreamily, and it was so sexy, he crossed back to her while the water heated. He wanted to touch her.

Stepping between her legs, he gathered her against him, flesh to flesh. She clung to him, wrapping her limbs around his waist. Her hair was still down, golden and curly against her back, tempting. So he indulged himself in what had become one of his favorite sights—her hair wound up in his fist.

A six-foot-long mirror spread out behind the vanity and Gage had a front row seat for viewing the gorgeous woman reflected there. Sensation engulfed him, sending a blast of blood to his groin so fast, it left him lightheaded. He groaned and his eyelids drifted shut. *No bueno.* There was no way in hell he was missing a minute of this.

Prying his eyes open, he gorged himself on the sight of the lovely naked woman in the mirror, and the man who was poised provocatively between her legs. And that's when he realized this was the first time he'd seen Cass fully unclothed. They'd made love in a couple of inventive spots that had been, oh, so very hot, but it hadn't given them the time to undress.

This was a first. And he planned to enjoy every second of it.

Reverently, he soaked her in. Then he was kissing her, delving into the moment with every fiber of his being. She made him ache, down deep inside where it couldn't be salved. Except by her.

They undulated together, physically and in their reflection. Steam from the shower gave the picture of the two of them a dreamlike quality, and it was the most erotic scene imaginable.

When they'd both shuddered to an intense, unbelievable release, he gathered her in his arms and took her to the shower, where he ministered to her like a slave doting on his mistress. It was as much an act of making love as what had happened on the vanity, though the thorough washing could never be remotely construed as sex. Didn't matter. Here in the shower as he rubbed soap over her skin and slicked shampoo through her hair, he wanted to make her feel as good as she made him feel, to connect on a higher level. Maybe somehow, he could open her up enough to know the ice was gone for good.

He couldn't stand it if things went back to being frozen between them.

Because he liked this Cass. More than he should. Far more than he had in college. This time was totally different, but he couldn't put his finger on what caused it to be that way. When he was inside her, his heart beat so fast, he thought it might burst from his chest, and when he wasn't with her, he thought about her. And not just about the physical stuff, though that was never far from his mind. No, he thought about how she'd come into her own as a woman. As a CEO. She'd grown far beyond his decade-old counsel.

The water grew cool and he shut it off, drying her tenderly. When he swiped the last of the water away, she grazed his cheek with her hand and lifted his lips to hers for the least suggestive kiss of his life. There was nothing sensual about it, just her laying her lips on his, and he couldn't have ended it to save his life.

Finally, she pulled back with a smile.

"Get dressed and let's eat something," he suggested, shocked at the roughness of his voice. He'd like to chalk it up to the explosive encounter on the vanity but that had happened thirty minutes ago. He suspected the source was Cass. Always Cass.

"Tired of me naked already?" she asked saucily.

"Never. I need nourishment if I want to have any hope of keeping up with you."

Dinner consisted of Chinese takeout eaten at the long island in Cass's kitchen. They sat on barstools, legs entwined and heads bent together as they laughed over failed attempts to use the included chopsticks.

Later that night, after a worthless attempt to watch a romantic comedy on Cass's wide-screen TV, he curled around her in her big fluffy bed, skin to skin. Moonlight poured in from the large triple bay window opposite the bed, where Cass had drawn the curtain to reveal the silvery lake. It was a million-dollar view but he only had eyes for the woman in his arms.

He stroked her hair, letting her essence wind through him and he had to know.

"Cass," he murmured. "Why did you agree to talk to the others about selling the formula?"

She stiffened and he regretted bringing it up. But weren't they at a place where they could be honest with each other? He hadn't sniffed out her agenda so far; the only thing he hadn't tried was flat-out asking.

"It doesn't matter. We haven't found the leak yet."

The bleakness in her voice reached out and smacked him. "We will. We'll spend all day tomorrow on it."

"Yes. We have to. Otherwise, I'll lose my job."

"What? They can't fire you. You own one-fourth of the company."

"Yeah," she allowed. "But if they say I'm out, I'm out. It's a vote of no confidence. I'd sell them my share and find something else to do with my life. That's the downside of being on a team."

He rolled her to face him in the dim moonlight. "You're not giving yourself enough credit. You've done amazing things with Fyra *because* you're a team."

He'd never been part of anything and he felt the lack all at once. Cass and her friends had been together for a long time. Longer than he'd known her. He'd never connected with anyone like that.

What would it be like if he did? If he hung on to someone longer than a couple of nights? Not as business partners, but as lovers. Would it always feel like this, like he felt with Cass? As though he could never get enough, never get tired of her, never run out of things to talk about?

It couldn't. Could it? Maybe for other guys who didn't have promises to their long-lost brothers to keep. Who would he be if he settled down?

She gave him a small smile. "Be that as it may, if I don't plug that hole, Fyra's profits could plunge. I have to answer to the whole company, as well as my executive team. Who are also my friends."

She was making herself accountable, like a great CEO should. It was inspirational and a little moving.

Her firm resolution spoke to something inside that he had no idea was there. Awed at the wash of emotion, he took in the serious expression on her beautiful face and everything shifted.

Cassandra Claremont wasn't just a fun distraction. He was starting to fall for her. How was that possible? He'd never let his emotions go like this. And what was he supposed to do with it—offer her his heart? Make her a bunch of promises?

Fall was definitely the right word. He'd fallen so far out of his depth, he'd need a thousand-foot ladder to climb his way out.

A bit panicked, he tried to get back on track. "So we'll find the leak. That's the only answer."

Get that squared away and then get the formula. That's what he was doing here. The crazy talk, that wasn't him.

He had nothing to offer Cass but a few laughs and a hundred million dollars. Then he'd go home and be done here. Like always. Like he was comfortable with.

She smiled. "Easier said than done, apparently."

"Double down, sweetheart." He kissed her temple. "I'm still a good bet. Get some sleep so we can spend all day tomorrow finding your name."

"I've heard that one before," she said wryly.

She'd meant it as a joke, but it sat heavy on his chest. He'd spent far more time focusing on pleasure than he had business with absolutely no thought to how their lack of progress might be affecting her. He could do better.

"Really. You can count on me. I promise we'll get there."

She didn't argue, though he understood why she might have a case for not believing in him.

As she drifted off to sleep, he gathered her in his arms and tried not to think about how natural it felt to be her go-to guy, how it made him want to stick to the problem until it was solved. How it made him want to stick to her.

Coupledom. Love. Living with someone under the same roof, sharing a bed, bank accounts—that was definitely an adventure Nicolas had never gotten to have. Gage had been avoiding anything that even remotely looked like that under the pretense of living life to the fullest on behalf of his brother. But in reality, the whole concept made him want to run screaming in the other direction.

Or at least it used to. He'd developed the strangest urge to stop running.

And he was truly daft if he thought for a moment that settling down was in the cards for someone like him.

Ten

A mournful howl woke Cass in the morning. She blinked. Sunlight streamed through the window and Gage's heavy arm pinned her to the bed.

Arwen apparently wanted them both to know she was awake and bored. But only one of them seemed to notice. Gage still slept like the dead, a fact she'd not forgotten. He'd never been the type to let the pressures of life keep him from something he enjoyed as much as sleep. He'd need a dictionary and autocorrect to spell *stress*.

One of the many reasons he fascinated her. It was a trick she'd like to learn. She openly evaluated his beautiful face, relaxed in sleep. How did he shut off everything inside so easily? Or was it more a matter of truly not caring and therefore, there was nothing to shut off?

The latter, definitely. She'd lost count of the number of times she'd labeled him heartless. It was starting to ring false. Any man who clearly loved his dog as much as Gage did couldn't be heartless. And he'd been so sweet in the Hummer yesterday before rocking her world, then again last night.

She shook her head. And therein lay his danger. Instead of uncovering his involvement in the leak, he'd uncovered *her*, in so many ways, reminding her why she'd fallen for him in the first place. He'd taken everything she'd dished out and come back for more.

He lulled her into believing he might be someone different this time around, someone who would be there tomorrow and the next day, growing closer as they grew older. Someone who could be trusted. She had no evidence of that.

Didn't stop her from yearning for it, though.

Gage stirred awake and smiled sleepily at her. "Morning, gorgeous. You better stop looking at me like that or we're going to get a very late start on our investigation. That's our top priority for today, no ifs, ands or buts."

"Oh, that's a shame. I do enjoy your butt." She snickered as he waggled his brows.

And somehow, she ended up under him and panting out his name before she'd scarcely registered him moving.

Finally, they rolled from bed at nine o'clock, the latest she'd gotten up since…college as a matter of fact. Gage was truly a terrible influence on her.

But then he took over her Keurig and brewed her a giant cup of coffee, exactly the way she liked it, which hadn't changed in a decade, but still. How had he remembered that? Trinity never remembered that Cass hated sugar in her coffee, and Trinity had watched Cass make it every weekday morning for years and years.

Gage elbowed her aside as she tried to put some breakfast together, insisting on scrambling eggs and frying bacon himself, despite never having set foot in her well-equipped kitchen before. Of course, she rarely set foot in it either. The pan he'd scrounged up from under the Viking range didn't even look familiar.

After Gage filled a plastic bowl with food for Arwen, they sat outside on the flagstone patio at the bistro set she'd purchased shortly after buying the house five years ago, and yet had never once used. It was a gorgeous morning full of fluffy clouds flung across a blue sky, but Cass was busy watching the man across from her as he tossed an old tennis ball he'd pulled from Arwen's bag. The dog raced after it time and time again. In between tosses, Gage shoveled eggs and bacon into his mouth in what was clearly a practiced routine.

It was all very domestic and twisted Cass's heart strangely.

She'd dated a guy... Tyler Matheson...a year or so ago and she'd have said it was bordering on serious, but she'd never once thought about inviting him to her house for the weekend. It had felt intrusive. As if men and her domain should be kept separate at all times. When they'd broken up, Tyler had accused her of being cold and detached, but she'd brushed it off as the ranting of a rejected man, just like she'd ignored the hurt over the unkind, unnecessary accusation during what should have been an amicable split.

Now she wasn't so sure he'd been wrong.

In contrast, Gage had flowed into her life effortlessly. As if he'd always been there and it was easy and right. As if they'd picked up where they'd left off. She'd been holding her breath for almost a decade, waiting for her heart to start beating again. And now it was.

She stared at him as if seeing him for the first time.

She'd never gotten over Gage Branson and chalked it up to having endured such a badly broken heart. But that wasn't it at all. She'd never gotten over him because she was still in love with him.

She shut her eyes for a beat. That was the opposite of a good thing. And this was a really bad time to discover it. He might be involved in the leak. Hell, he might have even orchestrated it and at this rate, she'd never find out. If he flat out denied involvement, she'd never believe him. He'd proven he couldn't be trusted personally, so what was to say he could be trusted professionally? She would not give him the opportunity to destroy her or her business all over again.

Even if he got down on one knee and proposed, which would happen when monkeys learned to pilot a stealth bomber, she'd say no. Her own self-preservation overrode everything.

"I did some more digging into our files. Ready to talk through them?" she asked after she cleared the emotion from her throat. Not only was it a horrible time to discover she still had very real, very raw feelings for him, it would be a disaster to tip him off. God knew what he'd do with it. Twist it around and say she owed him something.

He glanced at her, ball in hand, as Arwen barked to show her displeasure at the interruption. He threw it to the far end of Cass's property, a good hundred yards, and managed to make it look effortless. Like everything else he did.

"Sure. We've got all day and most of tomorrow. Let's make good use of it."

That was her deadline to somehow work through her emotional mess, too. A day and a half to get him out of her system for good and move on.

"I'm curious." She drank deeply from her coffee mug for fortification. "When I talked to you about planting false information, you seemed to know a lot about how digital forensics works. How did that come about?"

The best way to get him out of her system was to prove his involvement in the leak. Then she wouldn't have to remind herself he wasn't trustworthy. Because he'd be in jail. Her heart squeezed. Surely that wasn't going to be the result of all this.

But even if it wasn't, Gage's presence in her life was still because of the formula. He wasn't falling in love with her. He was only here to squash his competition.

Gage shrugged. "You learn stuff over the years. I read articles and such. But really, the reasons that wouldn't have worked are common sense."

Carefully, she raised her brows. "How so?"

"Because. Like I said, you don't have that kind of time. And you're assuming that the person responsible for the leak would actually be transferring files. What if they take handwritten notes? Memorize files? Take photographs? There are dozens of ways people can access information, especially if the person doing it is authorized in the first place."

All said very casually, while still throwing Arwen's ball. She'd watched him over her coffee cup, growing more frustrated by the minute at his clear hazel eyes and relaxed expression. He was supposed to be letting his guard down enough to say something he shouldn't.

Maybe he hadn't because she was being too subtle.

"Is that how you'd do it?" she asked, just as casually. Good thing she had a lot of practice at keeping her voice calm even when her insides were a mess. "Take photographs?"

"For what? To steal proprietary information?" He laughed and she'd swear it was genuine, not the kind designed to cover nervousness. "No reason for me to resort to underhanded tactics. If I want something, I buy it."

Yeah, as she well knew. Her coffee soured in her mouth. The problem with this line of questioning lay in the fact that she didn't have a clue if Gage was blowing smoke to distract her from his crimes or truly not involved in the leak.

How would she ever know for sure?

Maybe she was still being too subtle and the best way to resolve this was to flat out ask *Gage, are you involved?*

Surely she could read him well enough to recognize truth in his response. She opened her mouth to do it, once and for all, when his phone rang.

Frowning, he glanced at the screen. "Excuse me a sec. Someone from this number has called a couple of times but never leaves a message. Otherwise, I wouldn't take it."

Cass nodded as he stepped away from the table, her pulse pounding in her throat. So close. She'd almost blurted out the million-dollar question and she hated being forced to wait now that she'd made up her mind to go this route. But Gage ran a billion-dollar company. Of course people were vying for his attention.

She'd hoped to get her hands on his phone at some point this weekend, but snooping through his private life felt a little dirty, so she hadn't. So far. If he gave her any reason to, though…

Gage thunked back into his chair, his expression completely transformed from the relaxed, easygoing one he'd worn earlier. Thunderclouds had gathered in his eyes, turning his entire demeanor dark. "I have to leave. I'm sorry to cut our weekend short."

"What's wrong?" she asked before she thought better of it. They weren't a couple. They didn't share their problems. And no amount of yearning for that type of relationship would change things.

"Something's happened." Bleakly, he met her gaze, and suddenly it didn't matter if they weren't a couple. She reached out and captured his hand. In comfort, solidarity, she didn't even know. She just couldn't stop herself from touching him.

"What, Gage?" she asked softly, envisioning an accident involving his parents, a fire at his production facility. The pallor of his skin indicated it must be something bad.

"That was… I don't know for sure yet. I have to go home." He scrubbed his face with his free hand as he gripped Cass's with his other. "Someone I used to date died. Briana. That was her sister on the phone."

"Oh, I'm so sorry." Cass's heart twisted in sympathy. The woman must have been someone special for Gage to be so visibly upset. The thought of him caring about a woman so deeply set her back a moment. Was she missing something here? When had Gage become the committed sort?

"Thanks, I hadn't spoken to her in a long time. A year and a half."

Cass eyed him. "Then why would her sister have called you, if you don't mind me asking?"

Maybe *that* was the million-dollar question. Her curiosity burned. What if he truly had turned into someone who stuck around, growing close to this woman, and she'd been the one to dump him? Maybe *he* was nursing a broken heart.

After all, they'd never really talked about what the future between the two of them could look like. Maybe everything was within her reach if she just—

"She called because Briana had a son." Gage blinked. "My son. Or so she says."

* * *

Gage's two-story house overlooked Lake Travis just outside of Austin. It was one of the main reasons he'd bought the house several years ago and the water had always spoken to him. After driving straight home from Dallas in less than three hours—a record—he stood on the balcony, hands braced on the railing surrounding the enclosure and stared at the gray surface of the lake without really seeing it, wishing like hell the view didn't remind him of Cass.

But it did because her house was similarly situated near White Rock Lake in Dallas. He should be there with her right now, but wasn't because his world had shifted into something unrecognizable, where a paternity test was suddenly a part of his reality.

The woman who had called him was on her way over to discuss that very thing. It was bizarre. If what she'd said was true, he'd fathered a child with Briana.

Briana Miles. The name conjured up the image of a diminutive brown-haired waitress he'd met at a sports bar not far from his house. Beautiful girl. She'd come home to Austin after five years in LA and had started waiting tables so she could put herself through college, hoping to graduate without debt.

They'd struck up a conversation because Gage had expressed curiosity about how the University of Texas had changed in the almost ten years since he'd exited graduate school. That had led to a great couple of days that had ended amicably. He hadn't heard from her since.

The doorbell pealed through the house, and Gage opened the door to a short brown-haired woman with the swollen eyes and messy ponytail. Lauren Miles shared features with Briana and he could see their family resemblance even though he hadn't laid eyes on her sister in a year and a half.

"Come in," he said woodenly.

"The courier dropped off the results of the paternity test you took." She handed Gage the sealed envelope with her free hand. "I guess it's true that if you have enough money, you can get anything done quickly."

He ripped the envelope open and his vision went a little gray. No question. He was a father.

Lauren perched on his couch but he couldn't sit down, not until he got the most important question answered.

"Why?" he burst out as he absently paced the strip of hardwood between the couch and the fireplace. "Why didn't she tell me? I would have helped her with the medical bills. Paid for diapers and teddy bears. I would have—"

His throat seized.

Liked to be involved. But he couldn't finish the thought, not with the way his chest had gotten so tight that he couldn't breathe. All this time. Briana had been raising a baby without his help. Without even bothering to tell him he'd fathered a son. He'd have supported her if he'd known. She shouldn't have had to worry about anything.

And now it was too late.

Lauren bit her lip. "I argued with her about that. I really did. But she insisted you wouldn't want the baby and she was scared you'd make her have an abortion."

Gage's vision blacked out for a long minute. Rage tore through his chest and he thought he'd lose it if he couldn't punch something. *Make* her terminate her pregnancy?

Life was precious, so precious. That core belief was the one sole gift Nicolas's death had given him. The fact that Briana didn't know that about him infuriated him. Except how could he blame her? It spoke to the shallowness of their relationship that she'd assumed he wouldn't want his son.

Gradually, he uncurled his fists and breathed until he could speak.

"Fine, okay. I get that she didn't tell me because she—wrongly—assumed I wouldn't support her decision to raise her child. Nothing could be further from the truth. The baby is my responsibility and I appreciate the fact that you've come to me so I can do the right thing."

His vision went dim again as he processed what the *right thing* actually translated into. After years of cutting all ties with women as quickly as possible, one had managed to hook him with the ultimate string. For a guy who had no practice with commitment, he was about to get a crash course.

He was a father. A *single* father. His child's mother was dead and he had to step up. His carefree days of living life to the fullest had just come to a screeching halt with a set of brakes called parenthood.

And he'd never even held his son. What was he going to do?

All at once, he wished he'd asked Cass to be here with him. It made no sense. But he wanted to hold her hand.

"About that." Lauren scooted to the edge of the couch, brow furrowed as she leaned closer to Gage. "I'd like to formally adopt Robbie."

"Adopt him?" he parroted because his brain was having a hard time processing. Lauren wasn't here to pass off Briana's son to his father?

"That's actually why I contacted you, to discuss the paperwork that my lawyer is drawing up. You'll have to sign, of course, because you're the legal father on record. But it's just a formality," she said quickly. "I'm not asking for any child support or any split custody. He'd be all

mine and you can go about your life. I'm sure you're totally unprepared to be a father."

It was as though she'd read his mind.

Something that felt an awful lot like relief washed
through him. He'd give her money, of course. That was
nonnegotiable. But Lauren could pick up where Briana
left off and all of this would go away.

And the relief kicked off a pretty solid sense of shame.
"So you want me to sign away all rights to my kid?"

"Well, yeah. Unless Briana was wrong and you are
interested in being a father?" she asked tremulously, as
if afraid of the answer, and tears welled up in her eyes.
"You've never even met Robbie. I love him like my own
son. He's a piece of Briana and I can't imagine giving
him up. It would be best if he stayed with the family he's
always known."

"I don't know if that is best," he admitted and his stomach rolled.

He should be agreeing with her. He should be asking
her for papers to sign. Right now. What better circumstances could he have hoped for than to learn he had a
son but someone else wanted him? It was practically a
done deal.

But he couldn't. Somehow, he'd developed a fierce need
to see this kid he'd fathered. He needed it to be real, and
meeting his flesh and blood was the only way he could
sign those papers in good conscience.

"I didn't know my son existed before today," he heard
himself saying as if a remote third party had taken over
his body and started spitting out words without his per-
mission. "And you're coming in here like it's all already
decided. How can I know what's best for him? I want to
meet him first."

Gage had a significant number of zeroes padding his

bank account, which wouldn't be hard to figure out, even for a casual observer. This could still be an elaborate ploy for a seven- or eight-figure check. But he didn't think so.

She nodded once. "Can it be in the next couple of days? Briana didn't have much, but her estate needs to be settled. Robbie's future being the most critical part, of course."

Settled. Yeah, all of this needed to be settled, but unfortunately, this was the least settled he'd ever been. What an impossible situation. And he didn't have the luxury of shrugging it off like he normally did.

Grimly, Gage showed Lauren out and sat on the couch, head in his hands. And he didn't even think twice about his next move. He pulled out his phone and dialed Cass.

When he'd left her in Dallas, it was with a terse goodbye and a promise to call her, but he'd never imagined he actually would, at least not for personal reasons. It should have been a good place for them to break things off and only focus on the business of Fyra's formula. He'd planned for it to be the end, but nothing with Cass felt finished.

Besides, he needed someone with a level head who knew him personally to stand by his side as he met his son for the first time. Someone who wouldn't let emotions get the best of her. Someone he hoped cared enough about him to help him make the right decision. Someone like Cass.

Too late, he realized none of that actually mattered. He wanted Cass because *she* mattered. Yeah, it scared him, but he couldn't deny the truth. The formula had ceased to be the most important thing between him and Cass.

Cass answered on the first ring and he didn't even bother to try and interpret that. Too much had shifted since they'd last talked for petty mind games like guessing whether she'd missed him like he'd missed her. Or whether she'd realize the fact that he'd called her had earth-shattering significance. It did. She could do what she wanted with that.

"I need you," he said shortly. "It's important. Can you come to Austin?"

Eleven

Cass went to Austin.

There really wasn't a choice. Gage had said he needed her and that was enough. For now. Later, she'd examine the real reason she'd hopped in the car ten minutes after ending his call. Much later. Because there was so much wrapped up inside it, she could hardly make sense of it all.

When his name had come up on her caller ID, she'd answered out of sheer curiosity. You didn't drop something on a woman like a surprise baby and then jet off. Of course, she'd also been prepared for some elaborate plot designed to see her again so he could coerce her into either giving him the formula or getting naked, at least until he got tired of her again. She'd planned to say no and spend the weekend crossing the finish line on the leak's name.

She had to be close. The list of potentials wasn't *that* long.

But instead she'd found herself saying yes to the surprising request to accompany Gage as he met his son for the first time. He wanted *her* to be by his side as he navigated this unprecedented situation. The sheer emotion in his voice had decided it. What if Gage wasn't involved in the leak and she missed her chance to find out what might happen between them?

Cass held Gage's hand as they mounted Lauren Miles's front steps and wondered not for the first time if he'd literally come apart under her grip. The new, hard lines around his mouth scared her, but the fragility—that was ten times worse. As if the news he'd fathered a child had replaced his bones with dust. One wrong move and he'd blow away in a strong wind if she didn't hold on tight enough.

Just this morning, they'd been drinking coffee on her back porch and she'd been desperate to work him out of her system. So she could let him go and move on. Clearly that wasn't happening. But what was?

Less than four hours had passed since she received Gage's troubling and cryptic phone call and their arrival on this quiet suburban street. The slam of a car door down the way cracked the silence. It felt as if there should be something more momentous to mark the occasion of entering the next phase of your life. Because no matter what, Gage would never be the same. His rigid spine and disturbed aura announced that far better than any words ever could.

"I admire what you're doing," she told him quietly before he rang the doorbell. "This is a tough thing, meeting your son for the first time. I think you'd regret signing the papers if you didn't do this first."

The fact that he'd asked her to come with him still hadn't fully registered. Because she didn't know what it meant.

"Thanks." Gage's eyelids closed and he swallowed. "I

had to do it even though I feel like I'm standing on quicksand. All the time. I needed something to hold on to."

He accompanied the frank admission by tightening his grip on her hand. He meant her. She was the one holding him up and it settled quietly in her soul. In his time of need, he'd reached out to her. She wished she could say why that meant so much to her. Or why the fact that he was meeting this challenge head-on had softened her in ways she hadn't anticipated. Ways that couldn't be good in the long run.

But what if there was the slightest possibility that they might both put down their agendas now that something so life altering had happened? That hadn't felt conceivable in Dallas, but here…well, she was keeping her eyes open.

He rang the doorbell and a frazzled woman answered the door with a baby on her hip.

"Right on time," the woman said inanely, and she cleared her throat.

Gage's gaze cut to the baby magnetically and his hazel eyes shone as he drank in the chubby little darling clad in one of those suits that seemed to be the universal baby uniform.

"I'm Lauren," she said to Cass. "We haven't met."

"Cassandra Claremont." Since she wasn't clear what her role here was, she left it at that. She and Lauren didn't shake hands as there wasn't any sort of protocol for this situation, and besides, they were both focused on Gage. Who was still focused on the baby.

"Is this him?" he whispered. "Robbie?"

"None other." Lauren stepped back to let Gage and Cass into the house, apologizing for the state of it as she led them to the living room.

A square playpen sat off to one side of the old couch surrounded by other baby paraphernalia that Cass couldn't have identified at gunpoint. All of it was tiny, pastel and utterly frightening.

That was when Cass realized she knew nothing about babies. She'd always known they existed and murmured appropriately over them when other women who had them entered Cass's orbit. But this was a baby's home, where the process of living and eating and growing up happened.

Gage had told her in the car on the way over that the baby's aunt was seeking to adopt Robbie. Really Cass was floored Gage hadn't signed the papers to give up his rights on the spot. Why hadn't he? The solution was tailor-made for a billionaire CEO who thought commitment was the name of a town in Massachusetts. Give up your kid and go on living life as though it was one big basket of fun with nothing to hold you back.

Sounded like Gage's idea of heaven to her.

The fact that he was here meeting his son instead… well, she wouldn't have missed it for anything in the world.

Crossing to the mat on the floor, Lauren set the baby upright in the center of one bright square and motioned Gage over. "Come sit with him. I can't honestly say he doesn't bite, but when he does, it doesn't really hurt." She laughed without much humor. "Sorry, that was a lame joke."

Then Gage knelt on the mat and held out a hand to his son. The baby glanced at the stranger quizzically but then reached out and grasped his father's finger with a small baby sound.

Cass forgot to breathe as a wave of tenderness and awe and a million other emotions she couldn't begin to name broke over Gage's expression, transforming it into something that tugged at her soul. She almost couldn't watch as the moment bled through her, blasting away the last of her barriers against a man whom she could never call heartless again. It would be a lie.

His heart was all over his face, in his touch as he ruffled his son's fuzzy head. In the telltale drop of moisture in the corner of his eye.

She couldn't watch and she couldn't look away as her own heart cried along with Gage. That's what love looked like on him and she wanted more of it.

Thirty minutes passed in a blur as Gage held his son In his strong arms and laughed as the baby pulled at his father's too-long hair. He pumped Lauren for information, demanding details like what Robbie ate, whether he'd taken his first step, what he did when he rolled over. Robbie's aunt answered the questions to the best of her ability but it soon became clear she hadn't spent every waking minute with the boy like his own mother had.

A somber cloud spread over the four of them with its dark reminder that this wasn't strictly a happy occasion of father meeting son. Gage had a decision to make and he needed to make it soon so Robbie could get settled in the home where he'd live for the next eighteen years with his permanent parent.

Lauren announced it was Robbie's nap time. She left the room, disappearing into the back of the house to perform the mysterious ritual of "putting him down" and returned after ten minutes, her eyes puffy and red, as if she'd been crying.

"He's so precious." She sniffed. "It's so unfair. I can't tell you how it breaks my heart that he's lost his mother."

"It's hard for me, too," Gage admitted quietly. "My son should have a mother. Yet if Briana hadn't died, I might never have known about Robbie."

It was the most brutal sort of turnabout and it was definitely not fair play. But Cass couldn't argue that fate had set that pendulum in motion. And the swings had widened to encompass her, as well.

Gage held out his hand to Lauren. "Thank you for opening your home to him."

"I wouldn't have done anything else." Lauren shook Gage's hand solemnly and didn't let go as she caught his gaze to speak directly to him. "I love him. He's my nephew, first and foremost, and we will always share that bond of blood. But you're his father. That's something I can't be to him and I'm prepared for whatever decision you make. Please, take twenty-four hours, though. Make a decision you can live with forever."

Nodding, Gage squeezed Lauren's hand and turned to go, ushering Cass out the door ahead of him. His touch on her back was firm and warm and it infused her with the essence of Gage that she'd be a fool to pretend she didn't crave.

The best part was she didn't have to pretend. Instead of spending the weekend working Gage out of her system, something else entirely was happening and she couldn't wait to find out what.

He drove back to his mansion on the lake and helped her out of the Hummer, leading her up the flagstone steps to the grand entryway flanked by soaring panes of glass… all without asking if she planned to stay.

No way in hell was she going anywhere.

Throwing a frozen pizza in the oven passed for dinner, and an open bottle of Jack Daniel's managed to intensify the somberness that had cloaked them since leaving Lauren's house. They pulled up bar stools at the long, luminous piece of quartz topping the island in Gage's kitchen and ate.

Or rather, she ate and Gage stared into his rapidly diminishing highball filled with whiskey.

"I'd ask if you were okay," Cass commented wryly, "but that would be ridiculous under the circumstances. So instead I'll ask if you want to talk about it."

"He looks like Nicolas." Gage tossed the last of his Jack down his throat and reached for the bottle. "Robbie. He's the spitting image of my brother at that age. My mom had a shrine to her firstborn lining the hallway. Literally dozens of pictures stared down at me for eighteen years as I went between my bedroom and the bathroom. Today was like seeing a ghost."

"Oh, Gage." *More alcohol needed, stat.* Her own Jack Daniel's disappeared as she sucked the bottom out of her glass through a straw. "That's…"

She didn't know what it was. Horrible? Morbid? Unfortunate? Gage had talked about Nicolas in college on occasion, so she knew the tragic story well. It had shaped a family into something different than might have been otherwise.

"It's a miracle." A small smile lit up Gage's features. "I never would have imagined… My son is a gift that I don't deserve. A piece of myself and my brother all wrapped up into one amazing little package."

The love and tenderness she'd seen at Lauren's house when he looked at his son appeared again in his expression, and it pierced her right through the heart. It was breathtaking on Gage, a man she'd longed to look at *her* that way, a man she'd been sure didn't care about anything. The fact that he'd shown a capacity for it was a game changer.

And she had a strong feeling she knew what that look signified. "You don't want to give up Robbie."

Gage shook his head. "I can't. It never sat quite right with me anyway, but once I saw him… I don't need twenty-four hours to decide. He needs me."

He wasn't going to walk away from his son. And she'd never been more proud of someone in her life.

That burst Gage's dam and he started talking about Robbie. How was it possible that a man becoming a father before her very eyes could be so affecting? But it was. Gage's decision opened up a part of her inside that flooded with something divine and beautiful.

They drifted to bed where they lay awake, facing each other in the dark, as she listened to Gage's plans for his impending fatherhood. There was no subject too inane, from the color of the walls in his son's new room to what kind of car Gage would buy him when he turned sixteen.

Cass smiled and bit back a suggestion that he let his son pick out his own car. Far be it from her to interrupt his flow. This was his way of working through it and her job was to be there for him. It was nice to be needed by the one man who had never needed her. Heady even.

"Thank you," he said abruptly. "For coming on short notice. For holding my hand. For not heaping condemnation and a sermon on top of me. I had to figure this out and I couldn't have without you."

What, like he was expecting her to shake her finger at him and give him a lecture about accepting responsibility? She shook her head. "You're giving me too much credit. I just responded to a phone call. You did the hard part."

"No. I don't do hard." His voice went scratchy but he blazed ahead. "I get out before anything difficult happens. Back at your house, that was supposed to be about burning off the tension so we could focus. It wasn't supposed to be the start of something. I don't do relationships. You know that, right?"

That was the first time she'd ever heard him admit he had a commitment problem. Admitting it was the first step toward curing it, right?

"Yeah. I knew it wasn't anything more than sex."

"What if I want it to be?" he asked, sincerity warming his voice and curling through her in the dark. It was as if he'd read the same question in her heart and voiced it out loud.

"What if you do?" she heard herself repeat when she should have been saying *so what?* Or *this is goodbye right now.* "Have things changed?"

Please, God. Let that be true and not a huge mistake.

His hand found hers, threading their fingers together, and the rightness of it drifted through her like a balm. She could listen to him talk all night long if this was the topic.

If she hadn't gotten in the car when he asked her to come to Austin, she'd never have gotten to watch this monumental shift in Gage.

"So many things," he repeated quietly. "I'm not even sure how yet. The formula… I wasn't going to give up. I wanted it and I was going after it. But somewhere along the way, I started to want more."

The earth shifted beneath the bed, sliding away faster and faster as her mind whirled, turning over his words, searching for the angle, the gotcha. "What are you saying, Gage? That you want to keep seeing each other?"

He spit out a nervous laugh. "Why not? I like spending time with you. I'm pretty sure the feeling is mutual or I'm much worse at this kind of thing than I think I am."

"You have a lot going on right now," she said cautiously. "Maybe this isn't the best time to be talking about this."

"I *am* worse at this than I thought if I'm not making myself clear. Let's see how it goes. I'll come up to Dallas. You drive to Austin. We talk on the phone during the week. Maybe a video chat late at night that involves some dirty talk. I don't know. I've never done this before."

She could envision it. Perfectly. Sexting during a conference call and naughty emails and rushing to throw her overnight bag into her Jaguar for a Friday night dash to the Hill Country in anticipation of a long weekend in Gage's bed.

But for how long? And what would happen when he ditched her again, as he surely would? "I don't know how to do that either."

His sigh vibrated through her rib cage. "Yeah. Robbie changes everything."

That was so not what she'd meant. "Why, because you think you being a father is a turn-off? Think again."

"It should be. My life will never be the same. It's ridiculous to even say something like 'let's see how things go.' I already know where I'm going. Play dates, preschool, the principal's office and Cub Scouts."

He was committing to his child. Didn't that give her some hope he might want to commit to her, too?

"Maybe it's not so ridiculous." Had that just come out of her mouth? It was madness. But honest.

"Stop humoring me," he said flatly. "I get it. Everything is up in the air, which is unfair to you. Besides, you might want to think about whether you'd like to be in the same boat as Briana. I don't know how she got pregnant. I used protection every single time."

Yeah, that had occurred to her. But he'd gotten it wrong. She was in a whole boatload of trouble regardless because she wasn't mother material. She ran a million-dollar company for crying out loud. Any conversation she and Gage had about seeing where things could go included a future with a baby no matter what. Now that she'd thought of it, she couldn't *stop* thinking about it.

But there was no point in heaping condemnation on him, especially not when it sounded as though he was doing a pretty good job of that on his own. "Of course you did, Gage. It was an accident. It happens all the time, even to smart, careful people."

Her heart twisted as they talked about subjects that shouldn't be a part of his reality. Gage embraced this challenge in a way she'd never have guessed—the king of disentangling himself from anything that smacked of the long-term had changed when she wasn't looking. Really and truly changed, which she'd just spent a considerable amount of effort denying over the past week.

What if she *could* trust him with her heart this time? A world of possibilities might be open to her. To both of them.

It gave her a lot to think about.

In the morning, she awoke before Gage. His sleeping form was close enough to touch but she didn't dare do it. He'd only slept for a couple of hours last night, which she knew because she'd been holding him when he'd finally drifted off.

Their conversation had meandered to every subject under the sun—how they'd gone without their first year in business, what kind of spices you could add to ramen noodles to make them taste like something other than cardboard, the first splurge purchase they'd made when their companies finally turned a profit.

It was like the old days, except Gage hadn't even tried to kiss her. Last night hadn't been about sex, a fact she appreciated. But at the same time, she couldn't help but try to categorize the night.

A turning point, perhaps. But one thing she did know for sure—she had to answer that million-dollar question about Gage's involvement in the leak. Soon.

Twelve

Cass entered this new phase of her relationship with Gage with equal parts caution and greed. She soaked up every second of laughing with him over Robbie's antics as Gage visited his son at Lauren's house, and she helped Gage shop for nursery items.

No task required to prepare Gage to take custody of his son was too small for her involvement, apparently. She didn't mind. Except for the part where they never picked up the conversation about where things were going. Whether there was a goodbye in their future or not. Was she simply a hand to hold until he found his footing?

Eventually, that question would have to be answered. But she was content, for now.

She shuttled between Austin and Dallas enough times over the next week that she could pick out roadside elements as mile markers. That weed formation meant it was an hour and thirty-six minutes until she'd be in Gage's arms again. The pile of rocks by the exit sign meant she'd see Gage's beautiful hazel eyes light up at the sight of her in seventeen minutes.

In between, she ran her company and hired a private detective to look into the leak. If she hadn't been so distracted, she would have done so earlier. The move was enough to satisfy her partners into giving her more time. And enough to satisfy herself that if Gage was involved, she'd find out before things went too far. She hoped.

On Friday, one week after she'd snuck out early to get busy with Gage in his Hummer—totally by accident, in her defense—she spent an hour at the end of the day frantically whittling down her email in anticipation of spending the weekend in Austin with Gage.

Her phone rang. Speak of the devil.

"Hey, sexy," she purred.

"It's done," he said. "The last of Briana's estate is settled and Robbie is officially mine."

She swallowed. Hard. "That's great news!"

Just in time for the weekend. They'd expected it to take a few more days, but Lauren had been instrumental in pushing things through once she saw how serious Gage was about being a father. She could have made Gage's life a living hell and he'd said he was grateful she'd chosen to take the high road for Robbie's sake.

Except now it was real. Gage was a single father.

Now that the estate was settled, Robbie would come to live with Gage permanently. Lauren would still be a huge part of her nephew's life, and she and Gage had already discussed potential arrangements for holidays. Gage's parents had put their house in Houston on the market and planned to move to Austin so they could spend their golden years with their new grandson.

The only person who didn't have her future mapped out was Cass.

"So I guess Lauren is bringing Robbie over tonight?" she asked. She'd planned to drive to Austin tonight to spend the weekend with Gage.

Things had just come to a head. What did Cass know about dating a single father? If things progressed, was she really ready to be a mother? The thought frightened her. She had a demanding job. She couldn't be calm and cool around a baby. The timing wasn't great for any of this.

One step at a time. What better way to figure out what came next than to spend time with the man and his child?

"No, she asked if she could keep Robbie until Monday so she could say goodbye, just the two of them. I couldn't say no."

"That was sweet of you."

Her heart opened a little more with each glimpse of the man Gage was becoming as he met this challenge. Each time, she had to reprogram a bit more of her thinking. She wasn't sure what to do with the result.

"So instead of you driving here, I'm coming to you. You've already put far too many miles on your car in the past week. Turnabout is fair play," he reminded her in case she'd forgotten about his strong sense of tit-for-tat. "I'll be there in three hours."

She ended the call with a smile and drove home instead of to Austin. The reprieve gave her time to review the email she'd received a few minutes ago from the background-check company. They'd finally completed new scans of all her employees.

Thirty minutes later, she kicked back on her sofa with her laptop, the report and a list of cross-referenced employees who worked in the lab. The scans she'd ordered included arrest records, of course, but that wasn't necessarily a good indicator of someone's propensity toward corporate espionage. A better one was financial records such as property owned and debt, which was the section of the report where she focused her attention.

Someone with a mountain of outstanding bills might be a prime candidate for thievery, particularly in light of what the formula was worth to someone like Gage. He'd never buy it from a shady Fyra employee, but the culprit might not realize that.

But Cass knew that about Gage. The thought settled into her mind as if it had always been there. Of course that was true. Why would he have bothered to come to Fyra's CEO with an offer to buy the formula if he planned to buy it on the black market?

Or was she missing the big picture?

Everything was mixed up in her head and the addition of his new status as a committed father wasn't helping. She just didn't know whether she trusted Gage or not.

Cass refocused and noted two lab employees with outstanding mortgages that seemed quite large for what Fyra paid them. Also not a blinking sign that pointed to criminal activity. But a curiosity all the same, considering neither of them were married according to the scan. Inheritance, maybe, but Cass couldn't be too careful.

Next, she moved on to her employees' former employers and known associates. GB Skin leaped off the page almost instantly. Cass's gaze slid to the employee's name. Rebecca Moon. She worked for Harper as a lab analyst. She'd worked for Gage before coming to Fyra. Also in his lab.

It wasn't uncommon. Many of Fyra's employees had previously worked for Mary Kay, too. That didn't make them criminals, just people with skill sets companies in the cosmetics industry sought.

But no one from a competitor had approached Cass about her formula, except one.

Cass sat up and started from the beginning of Rebecca's report. The picture was not pretty. She had a wide swath of credit card debt totaling well over a hundred grand and outstanding medical bills from—Cass tapped the line once she found it—her ex-husband's many elective procedures. So Rebecca had gotten divorced but was still saddled with an ex's debt.

Shaking her head over the things people did to each other, Cass eyed the woman's known associates and a sense of foreboding grew in her stomach. All of the people linked to Rebecca had addresses in Austin. Not a big deal. The woman had lived and worked in Austin when she was employed by GB Skin.

It just seemed odd that Rebecca Moon hadn't made any friends in Dallas in the…seven months she'd worked for Fyra. Not one person from her new neighborhood had asked her to lunch via text message or friended her on Facebook?

The background check hadn't extended to Rebecca's friends' information. So there was no way to know if the people she'd interacted with online and made phone calls to were employed by GB Skin—but logic would dictate that she'd made friends at Gage's company and kept them.

If Gage had found that out somehow, would it have been a temptation to lean on that connection? *No*, she couldn't assume that. Could she?

Her stomach rolled again as she recalled how convenient the timing had been when he'd first shown up at Fyra. Yes, she knew the drive between here and Austin was easy. Someone could conceivably hop in the car with little planning and be here before lunch. It didn't mean Gage had known about the formula *before* the information hit the trade magazine, or that he'd used the leak as some kind of leverage to get her to agree to sell.

But still. Gage had been convinced Cass owed him something. But then he'd stopped reminding her of it. The formula rarely came up these days. Why, because he knew Rebecca Moon was going to steal it for him?

That was a stretch. But Cass couldn't get it off her mind. A leak was one thing, but the threat of the culprit doing additional harm was very real. As was the possibility she'd been played by the master, just like she had been in college.

She would drive herself crazy with that line of thinking. She used her time to thoroughly peruse the rest of the report but Rebecca was the only lead she had.

Who better to contradict whether he'd discovered the perfect mole in Cass's company than Gage himself? There was absolutely no reason she couldn't bring this information to him and get his explanation. They could be straight with each other. He'd talk to her and tell her she was being silly and then maybe she'd tell him that she'd hired a private detective. With the detective on the job, she and Gage could focus on each other. See what their relationship might look like with all the agendas put away.

Because if she couldn't trust him with business, what could she trust him with?

Halfway through the last page of the report, a knock on the door startled her. *Gage.*

She let him into her house and drank in the man's beauty and masculinity as she stood frozen in the foyer where he'd made love to her for the first time in a decade. A million powerful emotions washed over her. She'd tried to keep her distance. Tried to keep her heart where it belonged—in her chest and shielded from Gage—but as she looked at him, images flew at her, of him as he held his son, as he laughed with her, as he made love to her.

The addition of his baby had shifted things. Far more so than she'd have anticipated, and not the way she'd have thought. Gage was a father now. Did that mean he'd changed his thinking about commitment? Was he ready to find a woman to settle down with?

But he still said things like *let's see how it goes. We're having fun. You owe me. Turnabout is fair play.* He'd distracted her from the leak again and again with his talk of pleasure before business. Had he been afraid she'd find something?

Ask him about Rebecca. Go on.

The wicked smile he treated her to fuzzled her mind and then he swept her into a very friendly embrace that promised to get a lot friendlier.

She pulled away and crossed her arms over the ache in her midsection that wouldn't ease. This was why she shouldn't let her heart take over. Emotions only led to problems.

"That was fast," she said brightly.

He raised one eyebrow quizzically. "Not fast enough, clearly. What's wrong?"

"I'm hungry," she lied. Of course he'd picked up on the swirl of uncertainty under her skin. "I waited for you to eat."

"I had Whataburger on the way. I'll hang out with you in the kitchen while you eat something, if you want."

"Sure." Then they could talk.

Except she couldn't seem to segue into *by the way, did you happen to set up a deal with one of my employees to steal my formula for you?*

Gage sat on a bar stool and chatted about Robbie, absently sipping a highball with a splash of Jack Daniel's in it. As she woodenly ate a very unappetizing sandwich that didn't sit well in her swirly stomach, she couldn't stand it any longer. The best approach was to ease into it, perhaps.

"When are we going to check in with each other?" she asked during a lull in Gage's conversation. Because of course their relationship, the leak and the formula were all tied together. Without one, the others didn't exist, and it was time to get all of it straight. "About how things are going."

"Now?" he suggested mildly. "Is that what's bugging you? You don't have to dance around it if that's on your mind. How are things going, Cass?"

Right, jump straight to her as if she could possibly articulate what was going on inside. She made it a habit of pretending she didn't have any emotions and she certainly didn't spend a lot of time cataloguing them for others when she didn't fully understand them herself.

Besides, this was about Gage. About whether he'd planted a mole in her company. Whether he'd invented a relationship with her to get his hands on her formula. Whether he'd become a man she could trust.

She scowled. "I wanted to know how it was going from your chair."

He took in her dark expression without comment. "It's working. But it's only been a week and Robbie will be a big part of my life come Monday. So I guess I'm still seeing how things go."

And somehow, his perfectly legitimate response plowed through her nerves like water torture. "What does that mean? Once you become a dad, you might decide two is enough?"

It would be exactly what she'd been expecting. *Sorry, this thing between us has run its course.* That's what she'd prepared for.

His brow furrowed and he abandoned his drink to focus on her. "No, it means it's a complexity in an already shaky situation."

"Shaky how?" she whispered. "Do you have something you need to tell me?"

Oh, God, what was she going to do if he came right out and confessed? He was bound to have some kind of rationale, like he'd only planned to use Rebecca to gather information for leverage or he'd say that technically, he hadn't done anything illegal.

"Cass, you're trembling."

Clearly concerned, he tried to grip her hand but she yanked it away, whacking her nearly empty wineglass and sending it clattering across the granite bar. Gage, bless his honed reflexes, caught the stemware before it shattered on the travertine tile below, but the trail of wine across her light brown counters would stain.

Good. Something to occupy her hands while she gained control again. *No emotions*, she scolded herself. *Brazen it out. Don't let him know what's going on inside.*

"You didn't answer my question," she said, pleased at how calmly she delivered the statement. And how coolly she wiped up the spilled wine with careful, even strokes. "If our situation is shaky, what's making it that way?"

"The formula, for one. I was expecting you to tell me to go to hell when I called about Robbie. But you didn't." He watched her closely but she refused to meet his all-knowing gaze.

She would never have told him that. He'd needed her. Maybe she should have told him to go to hell twenty times since then, but dang it, she'd wanted to believe in him. In them.

Yes, it meant something that she'd come when he called. She'd been hanging around, thinking she'd hold on to her heart and dip one toe in, but really, she was pathetically, predictably wishing for him to fall in love with her. Just like last time.

But he'd given her no reason to trust him, no reason to believe that could ever happen. Becoming a father didn't automatically make Gage Branson someone he wasn't and that's why he wasn't suddenly spouting promises and pretty words. *Let's see how things go* was code for *I've found my Ms. Right-Now.* Until he got tired of her. Until something better came along. It was all fun and games until someone's heart got broken.

Or worse, until she found out exactly how good he was at keeping business and pleasure separate. A little thing like corporate espionage wasn't supposed to get between them while they were burning up the sheets.

Before she could argue the point, he skewered her with those gorgeous hazel eyes and she felt it all the way through her soul. He'd burrowed under her barriers, winding his way through her heart despite all her vows to refuse him entrance. At the end of the day, she was the problem here. Because against all odds, she *had* started to trust him in spite of it all. And she shouldn't have.

"You came when I needed you." He held her gaze and wouldn't let go. "And we fell into something that I was hoping would continue. I meant it when I said I wasn't ready for it to end."

The rawness in his voice sliced through her. She wanted to believe him. Believe *in* him. The past week had been so amazing and surprising and deep, and sex had only been a small part of that.

When had she lost her "it's only sex" mantra? When had this become a relationship and not just sticking to a man to learn his secrets?

Unfortunately, she could pinpoint it exactly. It had happened the moment she'd answered Gage's call and he'd said, *I need you.*

He'd ruined her for other men—Gage Branson was it for her. She realized that now.

And she had to know once and for all if she could trust him.

"Rebecca Moon," she blurted out and his expression darkened so rapidly that the rag fell from her suddenly numb fingers.

"Yeah, what about her?"

"So you admit you know who she is?" Cass squawked.

"Of course I do. She used to work for me," he acknowledged without a scrap of shame. "My company isn't so big that I've lost the ability to keep track of my people. Especially those who worked in Research and Development."

"Used to work for you?" she prodded. "But not anymore?"

Gage stood, unfurling to his full height a good three inches above Cass. He crossed his arms, leaning a hip against the bar casually, but his frame vibrated with tension.

"Since I'm pretty sure we both know she works for Fyra now, it sounds like you're the one who has something you need to tell me."

This was her opening. The other Fyra executives were counting on her to solve the company's problems and the last thing she wanted was for her team to accuse her of letting her feelings for Gage get in the way of justice. Alex, in particular, was already poised to lambast Cass. She had to pull this thread.

"I'm sure there's a rational explanation." She resisted the urge to back away. "But Rebecca's in a lot of debt and maintains contact with people in your area. You can see how someone might think that's a suspicious combination. It just looks bad, Gage."

"Bad how?" he asked softly. Lethally. "What exactly are you trying to say?"

The pressure of his accusatory expression pushed on her chest, stealing her ability to draw in air. He was going to make her spell this out. She swore. "Come on. You agreed to help me identify a probable suspect for the leak but have spent almost every second distracting me from that goal. Almost as if you wanted to steer me away from any evidence pointing to a name."

Of course she was the dummy who'd fallen for it. Half of the fault lay with her.

"You seem to forget that I had an interest in finding the leak, as well. The formula is worthless otherwise."

She waved it off. "Only if you don't have another way to get your hands on it."

"Cass." He huffed out a sigh of frustration. "We agreed you'd talk to the others about selling when we found the leak. We haven't yet. What other possible way would I get my hands on it?"

Did he think she was born yesterday? "Turnabout is fair play, right? That's what you said when you demanded I sell you the formula less than twenty-four hours after its existence was leaked to the industry. Tell me the timing is a coincidence."

"It's a coincidence." His knuckles went white as he contemplated her with clenched fists. "But you don't really think so, do you? You suspect that Rebecca's the leak and I'm pulling her strings like some kind of corporate raider puppet master. You think I've paid her to steal the formula."

"Well…in a nutshell, yeah." It didn't sound so concrete

coming from Gage's mouth and she wavered. He didn't look guilty. He looked furious. "Are you denying it?"

"Hell, yes." A muttered expletive accompanied the declaration. "Though why I have to is the real question here."

Instantly, her hackles rose. Was he that out of touch? "Really? It's confusing to you why I might have a problem trusting you?"

Obviously, he didn't see anything wrong with being there for her and giving her a place to get away from all the pressures of life, being understanding and strong and wonderful…and then taking it away at a moment's notice. Like he had the first time. "You dumped me in college like yesterday's trash with *no explanation*. I can't—"

She shouldn't have brought that up. Not now.

"No explanation?" He stared at her, his expression darkening. "Our relationship is one of my fondest memories, or I wouldn't have rekindled it. But it ended at the right time, once it had run its course. We talked about it. That's what I said."

"Oh, you said that all right. But you might as well have said, 'It's not you, it's me.' Either way, it's a lame line designed to brush off the person you're tired of." All of this had been bottled up for far too long. It came rushing out—the formula and the baby and *let's see how it goes* all muddled together into a big emotional mess she couldn't control. "Surely you didn't think it was an actual reason."

He'd broken her and she wasn't letting him do it again. Not personally. Not professionally.

"Wait just a minute." He threw up a hand as if to ward off the barrage of words. "We had a lot of fun in college. But that's all it was—fun. Are you saying you expected an opportunity to talk me out of it when I said it was time to move on?"

"No," she countered. "I expected that you'd figure out

you loved me as much I loved you and ask me to marry you."

She'd thrown up wall after wall to prevent a repeat of those feelings. Unsuccessfully. Because at the end of the day, that was still what she wanted.

And she knew now it was an impossible dream.

"Marriage?" The pattern of Cass's granite countertops blurred as Gage processed that bombshell on top of the Rebecca Moon accusation. "You wanted to get married? To *me*?"

Of all the things he'd thought about their time together, her in a white dress and diamond rings and…other together-forever stuff that he couldn't even fathom right now—none of that had ever crossed his mind. None of that had ever crossed his mind with *anyone*, let alone back in college when he'd just begun to spread his wings.

He'd vowed to himself, and to Nicolas, to have the quintessential college experience—drink a lot of beer, sleep with a lot of women, have a lot of esoteric conversations at coffee houses with foreign exchange students. No one got *married* in college.

He and Cass had totally different viewpoints on their history. How was he only discovering this now? *And* in the midst of a conversation where apparently, he was being accused of planting an employee at Cass's company. His temper simmered again, which was not a good sign. He never got angry. Mostly because he never had much of an emotional investment.

Looked as if he was going to experience yet another first with Cass.

"I guess this is news to you," she said and her voice broke.

There were no tears, no hard lines around her mouth,

but he could tell she was upset about their relationship ending. *Still* upset. The bitterness radiated from her and he caught it in the gut.

"Completely. Jeez, Cass. We were kids with our whole lives—our whole careers—ahead of us."

But that wasn't true now. If that was what she'd wanted then, what had she wanted this time around? The same? While he was trying to reconcile and explore these new, unprecedented feelings she'd evoked, had she been waiting for a proposal? The thought put his chest into a deep freeze and none of the beating and breathing that should have been going on inside was working.

She crossed her arms over her abdomen as if to protect herself. From him. "So what's different this time that makes you say things like *let's see how it goes*? Am I suddenly more palatable now that I have power and money? Or is my allure strictly related to your bottom line?"

His anger mounted. How dare she accuse him of not only consorting with a former employee to steal from Fyra but then playing other angles, too. As though he'd faked his attraction and feelings for Cass strictly because of her formula?

"My offer to buy your formula is legitimate and legal. And I didn't bring up extending our affair because of it," he told her truthfully.

Maybe the affair had started as a way to make sure the odds fell in his favor. But that had changed a long time ago. She had their relationship all wrong—the first one and the second one—and somehow he was the bad guy in all of this. As though she'd had expectations of him that he'd stomped all over and God forbid he be given a second chance.

"Then why?" she pushed, her expression darkening

more with each passing second. "Why keep seeing each other? Why not end it like you always do?"

Because…he had all these feelings he didn't know what to do with. Because he liked being around her. Because he couldn't imagine saying goodbye.

But all at once, he couldn't spit that out. Heaviness weighed down his chest. If they didn't say goodbye, what then? He wasn't marriage material.

"Yeah, that's what I thought," she said derisively when he didn't answer her. "You haven't changed. You're another broken heart waiting to happen."

Another broken heart? Something snapped inside.

All this time… Cass had been in love with him. And he'd broken her heart because he'd ended their relationship, despite never making any promises. No wonder she'd been so frosty and uptight at first. Obviously, their past had colored her agenda and explained why he could never put his finger on what she was up to. Why he could never find his balance with her.

"Are you still in love with me?" he demanded.

She laughed but it sounded forced and hollow. "Boy, someone sure packed their industrial-sized ego for this trip down memory lane. What do you think?"

That cool exterior was a front, one she did better than he'd credited, but he knew the Cass underneath it. Very well.

Sarcasm meant he'd hit a nerve.

"I think you didn't deny it." Eyes narrowed, he evaluated her.

Of course, that question would remain unanswered because, at the end of the day, she didn't trust him. And he was still angry about it. The unfounded accusations about Rebecca Moon still stuck in his craw and he was having a hard time getting them loose. "I guess I should have ended things. Especially if you're convinced I'm out to steal from you."

"It doesn't matter," she cut in swiftly. "We both know your interest in me starts and ends with my formula. So I'll make it easy for you. This…whatever it is…is over."

So that was it? Because of how things had ended between them the first time, she chose to believe that he was involved in the leak and didn't have any intention of listening to him. She was operating under a decade-old hurt and refused to give him an opportunity to explore what he wanted this time. That was crap and he was calling her on it.

"What if I asked you to extend our relationship because I want to see what happens when we don't end things right away? It's totally unfair of you to say *adios* when I'm genuinely trying to figure this out. Almost as unfair as accusing me of being involved in the leak with literally no proof."

She stared at him, her eyes huge and troubled. "Yeah, well turnabout is fair play, Gage. Spend the next decade thinking about *that*."

Thirteen

Gage drove back to Austin, his mind a furious blur. Cass had found the ultimate way to get him back for breaking her heart—by accusing him of betraying her.

Turnabout is fair play.

If it had happened to anyone else, he'd have appreciated the irony.

As it was, his chest ached with unprocessed emotions. If it wasn't for the layer of mad, he might understand what had just happened. But he couldn't get the heaviness in his chest to ease or the anger to abate. She hadn't believed him when he said he wasn't involved. Because she didn't trust him.

In Cass's mind, he was guilty simply because he hadn't fallen to one knee and declared undying love. Stealing a competitor's secrets was apparently as much a crime to her as not proposing. It was ridiculous. He cared about Cass. Of course he did. Who suggested they keep seeing each other? *Gage*. Who had called Cass when he'd been at his absolute lowest? Still him. Didn't she get that he'd been falling for her all along and had kind of freaked out about it?

Obviously not.

He'd given as best as he knew how. And his best wasn't good enough.

Fine. That was the way it should be, anyway. Clearly this relationship business wasn't for him. But what if that meant he couldn't be a father either? What if he was completely flawed in some way?

Gage spent the remainder of the drive home nursing his wounds and then drowned them in a quarter of a bottle of Jack Daniel's. He tried to go to bed, where it smelled like Cass and everything good and hopeful in his life, and that was the breaking point.

He vaulted out of bed, scaring the bejesus out of Arwen, who was enjoying the rare treat of sleeping at Gage's feet. Head cocked at a curious angle, she watched him throw on jeans but elected to stay put when Gage stormed from the room.

Twisting open the whiskey again, he got started on what was probably a vain attempt to drink enough to forget the stricken look on Cass's face when she'd said *this is over*.

He'd hurt her. He got that. But it had happened a long time ago. This was all on her and her inability to forgive and forget. There was no reason for Gage to reevaluate anything, yet here he was, doing it anyway.

He groaned and let his head fall into his hands. Who was he kidding? He'd screwed up, too.

Whether it was fair, whether he'd made mistakes with Cass due to his unquenchable desire to best his competition, whether Robbie made his life unduly complicated—

none of that mattered. He'd lost something precious and he missed her. Cass should be in his arms at this moment and she wasn't and it sucked.

Before he dissolved into an unmanly puddle of regret, he palmed his phone and flicked through pictures of Robbie. The boy's face was so reminiscent of Gage's brother, it was almost eerie. Genetics. That's all it was, not a message from beyond the grave.

He's going to be a handful.

Gage smiled. Yeah, his son was pretty great. What did Nicolas know about kids, anyway? It was a sobering thought. His brother had guided him for so long. Who would be the voice of his conscience now that Gage was moving toward something new and different?

You'll figure it out. After all, you already know what not to do.

He definitely knew that. Gage would raise Robbie with no boundaries. Carpe diem and full speed ahead, unlike how his own parents had raised him. If Robbie wanted to run with scissors, Gage would put plastic tips on the sharp ends and lead the way. If Robbie wanted to climb trees—or mountains—Gage would be behind him every step, ready to catch him when he fell.

He'd say yes to every "Hey, Dad, can I...?"

Mom and Dad didn't put restrictions on you to keep you from having fun.

Yeah, he knew that. They loved Gage, fiercely, even to this day, despite their disappointment that none of Gage's childhood limitations had resulted in a son who played it safe. He lived his life unapologetically, reveling in all the experiences Nicolas couldn't.

Like falling in love?

Gage drained the highball and flipped it over instead of

refilling it like he wanted to. When his conscience came up with gems like that, it was time to lay off the sauce.

Except the thought wouldn't go away.

For his entire adult life, he'd avoided anything that smacked of permanence. Even with Cass, who made him feel alive and amazing and as though he wanted to be around her all the time. He couldn't just come out and commit. Why?

Because he feared losing someone who mattered—like his parents had. God, why hadn't he ever realized that? With Robbie, it had been easy. There hadn't even been a choice in his mind. But he had control over whether he committed to Cass and he'd exercised it by walking out the door instead of fighting for what he wanted.

You live life to the extreme but it costs you. You have no personal relationships. No one to lean on. What are you going to do when parenting gets hard?

Gage frowned. His parents were moving here. His mom would give him advice.

The same woman you just vowed not to emulate when raising your son? Good thinking. Besides, don't you want someone to be there for you who gets you? Who's your equal? Someone you can count on and vice versa?

"Shut up, already. I get it," he muttered. "I messed up with Cass and instead of figuring out how to fix it, I'm sitting here arguing with a ghost."

But was it even possible to fix it? Cass's frozen routine was a safeguard against *him*, after all. He'd started their relationship solely with the intent of leveraging their attraction to get his hands on her formula, and she was forcing him to reap what he'd sown. Which was no less than he deserved. The rift between them was as much his fault as hers.

He'd wanted something more and had been too chicken

to lay it all on the line, disguising his thirst for Cass as a drive to beat the competition.

And by the way…if you've never done permanent, never been in love, never figured out how to sacrifice and be selfless, you know being a father will be that much harder.

His chest squeezed again. Nicolas was right. Gage's closest companions were Arwen and his conscience disguised as his long-gone brother. He had no idea how to do relationships. And he needed to. Gage couldn't be a good father if he flitted between commitment and freedom. He'd already realized that but now he knew how to fix it.

He had to learn how to stick. He *wanted* to. Cass and Robbie were both worth it.

Somehow, he had to prove to Cass that she could trust him this time. That he wasn't responsible for the leak.

He wanted Cassandra Claremont in his life, living it alongside him, giving him the ultimate experience he'd yet to have.

But as difficult as it was to admit, Gage had no basis for figuring out what it took to be a good partner or a good father. He'd never had a relationship before—with *anyone*, his family, a lover…what was different this time? What could he offer Cass to convince her to give him one last chance?

After a long night of tossing and turning, Gage sat up in bed as the perfect answer came to him.

Phillip Edgewood.

Cass frowned as she listened to the detective spout more rhetoric about how the investigation was ongoing, nothing concrete to report, blah, blah. She switched her phone to the other ear but the news didn't get any better.

At the end of the day, Rebecca Moon either wasn't the culprit or she had been very, very savvy about her movements over the past few weeks. Nothing pointed to the woman as the source of the leak, nothing pointed to a link between her and Gage, and Cass was tired of beating her head against this wall.

She was even more tired of missing Gage and wondering why she was beating her head against that wall, too. The man wasn't interested in a relationship—which she'd known from day one. She'd done everything in her power to keep her emotions out of it, trying to convince herself she was sticking to him like glue so she could keep tabs on him.

It hadn't worked. She'd fallen in love with him all over again thanks to those quiet moments when he was the man she longed for, who believed in her but didn't care if she wasn't strong and capable 24/7, who'd demonstrated his ability to commit to his son.

None of that mattered. She couldn't trust him and that meant they were through. Forever.

That hole in her heart? It was there for good.

It almost would have been better to find evidence that Gage had been the one whispering in Rebecca's ear. At least then Cass could hate him for being a sleaze. Instead, she'd had to cut ties because, after it was all said and done, he only cared about the formula. When she'd told Gage it was over, he hadn't argued. Because he knew he'd end things eventually, so why not now?

A knock on her open door dragged her attention away from the detective's disappointing phone call and the regret burning in her chest. Alex stood in the doorway. Cass waved in the CFO and held up one finger in the universal "give me a minute" gesture as she told the detective to keep digging.

Alex sauntered into her office, but Cass could tell this wasn't a friendly visit.

"We need to talk," Alex said before Cass had even set the phone on her desk. "The prelim quarterly numbers are not looking good."

Cass bit back the groan. When it rained, it poured. "And now you're going to tell me they're down due to the leak, right?"

The hard line of Alex's mouth didn't bode well. "I don't think we can directly pin it on that. But it's clear we've got a problem, and not having that breach buttoned up isn't helping."

The accusation of fault hadn't been verbalized but it came through loud and clear. This was all on Cass and Alex wasn't pulling any punches. As the CEO, the buck stopped at Cass's chair and she should have found the leak's name long ago.

Helplessness welled up and nearly overflowed into her expression.

Push it back. Her throat was already so raw from watching Gage walk out of her life that she hadn't thought it could get much worse. Turned out she was wrong.

"I'm working on it," she said smoothly. Or what she thought would pass for smooth, but Alex scowled instead of lightening up.

"You've been saying that for weeks. I'm starting to wonder whether you've got a secret agenda you've failed to share with me."

Oh, God. She'd landed in turnabout hell. This was shaping up to be a redo of the conversation she'd had with Gage last week, except she was the one in the hot seat.

Being accused by *Alex*, who had been Cass's friend for years and years. They'd suffered through exams together in college, through Alex's man troubles, and of course, Cass's singular experience with Gage. Later, she and Alex had worked around the clock together, poring over financial statements for places to cut and bonding through the difficulties of starting a brand-new company.

Except Alex was in Cass's office in her capacity as one-quarter owner of that company. It was her right to call Cass onto the carpet. But she did not have the right to make this about something other than Cass's inability to do her job.

"I don't have a secret agenda. Don't be ridiculous."

"Why are you always so dismissive of me?" Alex's unmanicured fingernails drummed against her leg in a restless pattern as she stared at Cass with a small frown. "I run this company alongside you, not beneath you."

Confused, Cass shook her head slightly.

There was more here than a reproach about Cass's performance on the job. This was personal. She did not get the lack of trust and animosity wafting in her direction. It wasn't as though she'd done something horrible to her friend that would make all of this justified. Not like what Gage had done to Cass, for example.

"What are you talking about?" Cass asked. "I'm not dismissing you. I—"

A brisk knock at the door cut off the rest and Cass glanced up sharply to see Melinda, Fyra's receptionist, hovering in the hall outside her office, practically wringing her hands.

"Sorry to interrupt." Melinda's eyes were so wide, it was a wonder they didn't fall out of her head. "But not really. You've got a visitor and, well, he's not the kind of person you make wait around. Besides, I'm afraid he's disrupted the entire office and I thought—"

"Who's the visitor?" Cass asked as patiently as possible.

The timing was the worst and whoever it was could wait. She wanted to get to the bottom of what was going on with Alex, once and for all.

"Phillip Edgewood," Melinda blurted out. There might have even been swooning. "*The* Phillip Edgewood. The *senator*," she stage-whispered in case Alex and Cass lived under a rock and might not know the popular United States senator. "He's even dreamier in person than he is on TV. Oh, and Mr. Branson is with him."

Cass stood so fast, her chair shot across the low-pile carpet and crashed into the wall. "You could have told me that first. Send him back right away."

A compact. There was a compact around here somewhere. Pulse thundering, Cass fished blindly through her desk drawer, fingers closing around three lipstick tubes, a bottle of Fyrago perfume and then a foundation brush before she finally located the powder case. She flicked it open and used the mirror to slick on a fresh layer of lipstick, which predictably went on crooked because of how badly her hand was shaking.

Gage was here. In this building. He'd come to apologize, to throw himself at her feet. To declare his undying love…

Now *she* was the one being ridiculous. Her heart deflated. Gage wouldn't have shown up after a week of radio silence with a US Senator in tow if he was here to step back into her life. He was here about the formula.

Business. Of course. The man separated business and pleasure like a pro.

"Hot date?" Alex asked wryly and Cass peeked over the compact.

God, she'd forgotten all about Alex and, lucky girl, she was about to witness Cass's complete breakdown.

"Actually, Gage and I aren't seeing each other anymore. We—"

He swept into the room and she forgot to breathe. The sharp, dark navy suit he wore would make an Italian tailor weep. His too-long hair was somewhat tamed and smoothed back, leaving his gorgeous face the focal point it should be.

She scarcely noticed the handsome dark-haired man at his elbow. Because next to Gage, Phillip Edgewood might as well have been invisible.

"Ms. Meer." Gage nodded to Alex as she rose. "This is my cousin, Phillip Edgewood. Phillip, Alexandra Meer, Fyra's chief financial officer."

The CFO and the senator shook hands politely, exchanging pleasantries while Cass shot Gage a look and hissed under her breath, "Senator Edgewood is your *cousin*? Since when?"

"Since I was born?" he suggested mildly. "His mother and my mother have been sisters for almost sixty years."

"You never mentioned that."

He shrugged, messing up the lines of his gorgeous suit, which was a shame. "I never mentioned a lot of things. Which, not so coincidentally, is why I'm here."

With that cryptic comment hanging in the middle of everything, Gage repeated the introductions between Cass and Phillip and swung his attention back to Cass. "Phillip has graciously agreed to help Fyra navigate the FDA process required to get your formula to market. I came by with him today so you could meet him personally and get the ball rolling. Oh, and he'll also help you grease the wheels at the patent office. The sooner you get going, the sooner the leak will become a nonissue."

Cass's mouth fell open. "We're not—I mean…what?"

"That's amazing, Gage," Alex said, with a withering glance at Cass. To the senator, she said simply, "Thank you. We're honored to have such expert assistance."

"Yes, of course." Cass nodded woodenly, her faculties still scattered. "Thank you. We appreciate the assistance."

And now she sounded like a parrot instead of a savvy executive. Gage *still* fuzzled her mind.

The senator smiled at Alex, and it took over his entire body, as if he was lit from within. Charisma radiated from him like the corona around the sun. Cass started to get an inkling of what the fuss over him was all about.

"It's no problem," Phillip said, but he was looking at Alex as if Cass didn't exist. "Is there somewhere we can go to talk? And of course, we should include your chief science officer."

"Dr. Harper Livingston," Alex interjected, and the two of them were off, their conversation deep in the details.

Looked as if Alex was more than willing to stay in the senator's orbit, though he was hardly her type. They were a study in contrasts with Alex's face bare of cosmetics and clad in a gray shirt and jeans. Senator Edgewood wore Armani and power, and not necessarily in that order.

They excused themselves to Alex's office, leaving Gage and Cass staring at each other.

"What was that all about?" Cass demanded. "Waltzing in here with a US senator and throwing him at Fyra like some kind of peace offering."

"You say that like it's a bad thing." Gage shoved his hands in his pockets. "Does that mean it didn't work?"

"That's what it was?" A little stunned, Cass sank into her chair. She'd been about to grill him on his angle. Without reason apparently. "A peace offering?"

"Yeah. I needed an 'in,' in case you wouldn't see me otherwise. Phillip was my trump card." He grinned and she fought to keep from smiling back. Too many unanswered questions for that.

"But why did you ask him to work with us on the FDA process? If we file for approval, that's a pretty clear indication we're not going to sell it. To you or anyone."

"That's why I did it. I don't want your formula anymore, but this seemed like the only way you'd believe me. Now it's not a factor between us." He took her hand and held it without making any other move, but that alone connected them. "I owe you, and turnabout is fair play."

"You owe *me*?" She shook her head, still dazed. "You've got that backward. You've been quite clear that it's the other way around."

"That was before I fell in love with you."

Her breath caught and she drank in the emotion spilling from his gaze. Love. Tenderness. All of the things she'd witnessed in his expression when he looked at his son. The same emotion she'd dreamed of seeing directed at her. And now it was.

Shell-shocked, she stared at him. "I…what?"

"Oh, am I stuttering again? Let me start over."

He swept her into his arms and laid his lips on hers, infusing his warmth into her dark and frozen soul. Everything thawed instantly, blooming under his talented mouth as he kissed her senseless. All of her feelings for this man surged to the surface, spilling out of her heart in an endless flow. He was in love with her, and all of the sharp, painful places inside smoothed out as she united with him, body and soul.

No. No, no, no. She wiggled away, breathless and still fuzzled because, *oh my God*, she wanted to dive back in and forget the past miserable week had happened. But it *had* happened.

"When did you decide this?" she demanded, but he just grinned and yanked her back into his embrace.

"For such a smart lady, you're being very slow to catch on," he murmured into her ear. "I'm not letting you go again. So you might as well forget about throwing up your walls. I'll keep knocking them down until you admit you're in love with me, too."

"Why would I do that?" She scowled but he just kissed the line between her brows.

"Because I'm sticking around this time. Forever," he promised and crossed his heart, catching her gaze. The depths of sincerity in his expression put a slow tingle in her midsection. "And I'd like to know up front where we stand. No seeing how it goes. No agendas. Just two people in it for the long haul."

"That's not what you want." Eyeing him suspiciously, she tried to cross her arms, but he wouldn't loosen his grip on her waist enough to give her room. "You want the formula, not me. So what exactly is all this Gage-speak supposed to mean?"

He pursed his lips and contemplated her. "Here's the thing. I haven't given you any reason to trust me. So I've spent the past week convincing Phillip to clear his schedule, and then I cleared mine. Because I want you to go to market with your formula so we can compete head-to-head. May the best CEO win."

That sounded more like Gage. There was a gotcha in there somewhere. A yet-to-be-named angle she couldn't see. "Now you're just talking crazy."

"No, I'm finally sane, thanks to you." Tenderly, he tucked a chunk of hair behind her ear. "You *have* moved past my mentorship. Far past. And turnabout is fair play. Show me what you've learned since then. I fully expect you to win."

It was as if he'd opened her heart and read the words she'd longed for him to say like a script. Where was this stuff coming from? Because if he kept going, she was going to completely lose all her safeguards against a bad decision.

But it was far, far too late for that. She'd been sliding toward Gage since the moment she'd recognized him in the parking lot of her building.

"Oh, I see." She didn't. But she had to keep fishing. His real agenda was buried in these well-delivered lines somewhere. "You've given up your bid for the formula and forgiven the debt you've claimed I owe you. Out of the goodness of your heart."

"That debt never existed." His small smile wiped the one from her face. "In fact, I owe you. Because I didn't know I had such a bad habit of turning a blind eye to what was happening around me. Briana had a baby without me cluing in. You were in love with me and I didn't know. You didn't tell me because I was too busy pushing you away. And then when you did tell me, I handled everything wrong. I should have admitted I was falling for you then. But instead, I clung to my freedom, not realizing it was meaningless. I'm a serial idiot."

This couldn't be real. All her dreams of being with Gage forever were not on the brink of coming true. Her life was not a fairy tale and he was not the guy he was claiming to be.

"So you've climbed aboard the commitment train?" She shook her head. "I'm sorry, Gage, but I can't buy that."

"Then you're going to feel very silly once I do this."

He pulled a small box from his jacket pocket and flipped the hinged lid to reveal something that might look like a diamond ring to someone whose vision wasn't instantly blurry with tears.

His arm dropped from her waist and he pulled the band from its velvet nest to slide it on her finger. "That's the sound of the conductor yelling 'All aboard.' I love you and I want to marry you."

She went a little lightheaded. "You know that if the

senator is helping us get the formula to market, marrying me won't get you access to it, right?"

Gage just smiled. "No agendas here. Mine *or* yours. You know if you marry me, you have to trust me. No more dates where you pump me for information, or sleepover games designed to figure out my angle. When you have questions, we have to talk about things like rational adults. And when we spend time together, it'll be because we can't be apart."

Guilt crushed through her chest. "Did you know the whole time?"

"No. I figured out later that all the strange questions were because you suspected I was involved in the leak from the very beginning. It's okay. I realized why you thought that was necessary. I hadn't given you any reason to trust me, which I hope I'm fixing right now."

Finally, it started to sink in. He'd taken soul-searching to a whole other plane. And somehow figured out how to claim her heart in the process with a simple thing like forgiveness. She'd held him at arm's length, convinced he would break her heart, when instead he'd offered his up with no strings attached.

She shoved back the flood of emotion for a second time. Or was it a third? She'd lost count because he'd done exactly what he'd predicted he would—knocked down her barriers against him.

"No agenda," she repeated dumbly. "Then why *marriage*? You could hardly say the word the last time this came up."

He took that with surprising grace and nodded. "I've spent years running from anything that smacked of commitment under the guise of living life to the fullest and experiencing new heights. I've done it all, except one thing. You're my ultimate experience, Cass. Just you. Everything feels better when I'm with you. Why would I keep running from that?"

"Because you're a serial idiot?" she choked out, and he laughed, pulling one from her, as well.

That was the benefit of falling in love with a man like Gage. She was botching up his marriage proposal and he still managed to pull it off.

"I am a serial idiot. I hope that means we're a perfect match," he said, his voice clogged with emotion she'd never heard before. "Because it would be dumb of you to take a chance on me. I'm going to immediately drop a baby in your lap. That's a lot to ask. I get that. But if you hand me that ring back, I'm only going to keep coming around until you say yes."

It was real. The man she loved had just asked her to marry him. She curled her hand around the ring, holding it tight against her palm. "The best thing about us is that we're equals. Guess that means I'm a serial idiot, too, because I never fell out of love with you."

Yes, clearly she'd gone mad because she never would have imagined admitting that in a million years. Never imagined being a mother. Never imagined she'd be this happy.

Strangely, Gage becoming a father had been the tipping point. She could trust that he'd stick around this time because she'd seen what he was capable of with Robbie. What it looked like when he loved someone. She knew it was possible and could finally believe it was happening to her.

A smile split his face and when he kissed her, he nearly split her heart, as well. Good thing. All the emotion inside was too big to be contained in that little bitty organ. Looked like she was getting her happily-ever-after.

Epilogue

Phillip Edgewood threw a hell of party. His status as one of the nation's most eligible bachelors coupled with his deep Texas roots afforded him a wide circle of acquaintances. Gage had never socialized with his cousin. Shame it had taken him so long to reach out to a man he'd known since childhood. They'd had lunch a couple of times since that day Gage had shown up out of the blue to ask for help, and they might even be on the way to becoming friends.

But tonight, Gage only had eyes for his date. Cassandra Claremont put the Hollywood celebs, Texas oil royalty and glittery society wives in attendance at Phillip's fundraiser to shame.

And Gage had been apart from his fiancée for five long minutes. He crossed the crowded ballroom to the bar, where Cass laughed over something Alex had said. That was a welcome sight. Cass had mentioned she and Alex were at odds over Fyra's strategy and that Alex had been the main one speaking out against Cass's leadership.

Whatever had happened to cause the rift appeared to be repaired, which Gage knew was a load off Cass's mind.

"Ladies," he murmured as he came up behind the most gorgeous woman in the room, wrapping his arm around her.

He couldn't touch her enough. Sometimes he did it just to assure himself he hadn't invented this fantasy out of thin air. But every time he reached out, she reached back. Commitment had its perks. Lots of them.

"Alex, you look fantastic," he commented truthfully as Cass's arm circled his waist in kind. "Did you do something different?"

Cass smacked him playfully. "Spoken like a true man. Of course she did. It's a formal party and we spent two days getting ready for it."

The two women exchanged smiles and piqued Gage's interest. "Sounds like there's a story there."

He'd been privy to nothing as Cass had told him to butt out. Repeatedly.

"A boring one," Alex assured him with a careful nod, likely in deference to the gravity-defying swept-up hairdo that drew attention to her lovely face. "Cass volunteered to give me a makeover, that's all."

"That's all?" Cass squealed incredulously. To Gage, she said, "The woman works for a cosmetics company and never wears the stuff. So I taught her a few tricks and voilà."

Alex blushed becomingly. "It's not that I didn't want to wear makeup. But every time I did, I felt like I was trying too hard."

Phillip appeared at Alex's side, which was the most likely cause of her blush. They made a cute couple and Phillip deserved some happiness after the untimely death of his wife several years before. Of course, the senator and the CFO both brushed off their association as "working together" to secure Fyra's FDA approval. They weren't fooling anyone.

As their host whisked Alex off to the dance floor, Gage nestled his fiancée closer.

"So things are good between you now?" he asked.

Cass nodded. "Yeah. We had a heart-to-heart and she admitted she was feeling left out. I have a tendency to deal with issues on my own, and apparently that comes across as...cold."

Gage stuck his tongue in his cheek. "You don't say."

"No, really," she insisted, oblivious to Gage's sarcasm. "I was acting like the title of CEO meant I had to do it all with no help and as if letting anyone see that I was uncertain was like some big crime. I ended up confessing that to all the girls when I told them I hadn't found the leak and you weren't involved. It was a real turning point and now we're 100 percent united. I have you to thank for helping me learn that."

"Me?" That was a genuine surprise. "You're the one who's been mentoring me in how to do this long-term thing. What did I teach you?"

"That it's okay to use your head and your heart." She smiled. "In all things. I couldn't have fathomed becoming a mother otherwise."

Robbie had warmed to Cass instantly, so much so that his son cried inconsolably when Cass had to go back to Dallas on Sunday nights. It was only temporary until they could figure out the logistics of moving an entire company's headquarters. And until they finished arguing about whose company was doing the moving.

"I told you we're a perfect match," Gage insisted. "I don't know what took you so long to get wise to how good we are together."

Guess it turns out you can live life to the fullest with one woman, after all.

Gage smiled. Nicolas was right once again. Cass was the ultimate experience and he couldn't wait to get started on forever.

* * * * *

*If you loved this novel,
don't miss the next book in
the LOVE AND LIPSTICK series
by Kat Cantrell*

A PREGNANCY SCANDAL

Available June 2016!

*And pick up these other sexy and emotional reads
by Kat Cantrell*

*THE THINGS SHE SAYS
MARRIAGE WITH BENEFITS
THE BABY DEAL
PREGNANT BY MORNING*

Only from Harlequin Desire!

*If you're on Twitter, tell us what you think of
Harlequin Desire! #harlequindesire*

#2449 REDEEMING THE BILLIONAIRE SEAL
Billionaires and Babies • by Lauren Canan
Navy SEAL Chance Masters is only back on the family ranch until his next deployment, but can the all-grown-up girl next door struggling to raise her infant niece convince him his rightful place is at home?

#2450 A BRIDE FOR THE BOSS
Texas Cattleman's Club: Lies and Lullabies
by Maureen Child
When Mac's overworked assistant quits, he's left floundering. But when she challenges the wealthy rancher to spend two weeks not working—with *her*—he soon realizes all the pleasures he's been missing...

#2451 A PREGNANCY SCANDAL
Love and Lipstick • by Kat Cantrell
One broken rule. One night of passion. Now...one accidental pregnancy! A marriage of convenience is the only way to prevent a scandal for the popular senator and his no-frills CFO lover—until their union becomes so much more...

#2452 THE BOSS AND HIS COWGIRL
Red Dirt Royalty • by Silver James
Clay Barron is an oil magnate bred for great things. Nothing can stop his ambition—except the beautiful assistant from his hometown. Will his craving for the former cowgirl mean a choice between love and success?

#2453 ARRANGED MARRIAGE, BEDROOM SECRETS
Courtesan Brides • by Yvonne Lindsay
To prepare for his arranged marriage, Prince Thierry hires a mysterious beauty to tutor him in romance. His betrothed, Mila, mischievously takes the woman's place. But as the prince falls for his "forbidden" lover, Mila's revelations will threaten all they hold dear...

#2454 TRAPPED WITH THE MAVERICK MILLIONAIRE
From Mavericks to Married • by Joss Wood
Years ago, one kiss from a hockey superstar rocked Rory's world. Now Mac needs her—as his live-in physical therapist! Despite their explosive chemistry, she keeps her hands off—until one hot island night as a storm rages...

———————

REQUEST YOUR FREE BOOKS!

2 FREE NOVELS PLUS 2 FREE GIFTS!

Ⓗ HARLEQUIN®

Desire

ALWAYS POWERFUL, PASSIONATE AND PROVOCATIVE

YES! Please send me 2 FREE Harlequin® Desire novels and my 2 FREE gifts (gifts are worth about $10). After receiving them, if I don't wish to receive any more books, I can return the shipping statement marked "cancel." If I don't cancel, I will receive 6 brand-new novels every month and be billed just $4.55 per book in the U.S. or $5.24 per book in Canada. That's a savings of at least 13% off the cover price! It's quite a bargain! Shipping and handling is just 50¢ per book in the U.S. and 75¢ per book in Canada.* I understand that accepting the 2 free books and gifts places me under no obligation to buy anything. I can always return a shipment and cancel at any time. Even if I never buy another book, the two free books and gifts are mine to keep forever.

225/326 HDN GH2P

Name	(PLEASE PRINT)

Address	Apt. #

City	State/Prov.	Zip/Postal Code

Signature (if under 18, a parent or guardian must sign)

Mail to the **Reader Service:**

IN U.S.A.: P.O. Box 1867, Buffalo, NY 14240-1867
IN CANADA: P.O. Box 609, Fort Erie, Ontario L2A 5X3

Want to try two free books from another line?
Call 1-800-873-8635 or visit www.ReaderService.com.

* Terms and prices subject to change without notice. Prices do not include applicable taxes. Sales tax applicable in N.Y. Canadian residents will be charged applicable taxes. Offer not valid in Quebec. This offer is limited to one order per household. Not valid for current subscribers to Harlequin Desire books. All orders subject to credit approval. Credit or debit balances in a customer's account(s) may be offset by any other outstanding balance owed by or to the customer. Please allow 4 to 6 weeks for delivery. Offer available while quantities last.

Your Privacy—The Reader Service is committed to protecting your privacy. Our Privacy Policy is available online at www.ReaderService.com or upon request from the Reader Service.

We make a portion of our mailing list available to reputable third parties that offer products we believe may interest you. If you prefer that we not exchange your name with third parties, or if you wish to clarify or modify your communication preferences, please visit us at www.ReaderService.com/consumerchoice or write to us at Reader Service Preference Service, P.O. Box 9062, Buffalo, NY 14240-9062. Include your complete name and address.

HD15

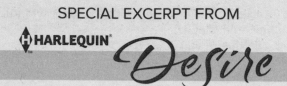
It had been a long day, but a good one.

Andi was feeling pretty smug about her decision to
quit her job and deliberately ignoring the occasional
twinges of regret. She should have done it three years
ago. As soon as she realized she was in love with a man
who would never see her as more than a piece of office
equipment.

Her heart ached a little, but she took another sip of
wine and purposefully drowned that pain. Once she was
free of her idle daydreams of Mac, she'd be able to look
around, find a man to be with. To help her build the life
she wanted so badly.

Her arms ached from wielding a paint roller, but
working on her home felt good. So good, in fact, she didn't
even grumble when someone knocked on the front door.

Wineglass in hand, she answered the door and jolted when Mac smiled at her.

"Mac? What're you doing here?"

"Hello to you, too," he said and stepped past her, unasked, into the house.

All she could do was close the door and follow him into the living room.

He turned around and gave her a quick smile that had her stomach jittering in response before she could quash her automatic response. "The color's good."

"Thanks. Mac, why are you here?"

"I'm here because I wanted to get a look at what you left me for." His gaze fixed on her and for the first time, he noticed that she wore a tiny tank top and a silky pair of drawstring pants. Her feet were bare and her toenails were painted a soft blush pink. Her hair was long and loose over her shoulders, just skimming the tops of her breasts.

Mac took a breath and wondered where that flash of heat had come from. He'd been with Andi nearly every day for the past six years and he'd never reacted to her like this before.

Now it seemed to be all he could notice.

Don't miss
A BRIDE FOR THE BOSS
by USA TODAY *bestselling author Maureen Child,*
available June 2016 wherever
Harlequin® Desire *books and ebooks are sold.*

www.Harlequin.com

Whatever You're Into… Passionate Reads

Looking for more passionate reads from Harlequin®?
Fear not! Harlequin® Presents, Harlequin® Desire and
Harlequin® Blaze offer you irresistible romance stories
featuring powerful heroes.

Do you want alpha males, decadent glamour and jet-set
lifestyles? Step into the sensational, sophisticated world of
Harlequin® Presents, where sinfully tempting heroes ignite a
fierce and wickedly irresistible passion!

♥HARLEQUIN® *Desire*

Harlequin® Desire novels are powerful, passionate and
provocative contemporary romances set against a backdrop of
wealth, privilege and sweeping family saga. Alpha heroes with
a soft side meet strong-willed but vulnerable heroines amid a
dramatic world of divided loyalties, high-stakes conflict and
intense emotion.

♥HARLEQUIN® *Blaze*

Harlequin® Blaze stories sizzle with strong heroines and
irresistible heroes playing the game of modern love and lust.
They're fun, sexy and always steamy.

Be sure to check out our full selection of books
within each series every month!

www.Harlequin.com

JUST CAN'T GET ENOUGH?

Join our social communities
and talk to us online.

You will have access to the latest
news on upcoming titles and special
promotions, but most importantly,
you can talk to other fans about your
favorite Harlequin reads.

Harlequin.com/Community

 Facebook.com/HarlequinBooks

Twitter.com/HarlequinBooks

Pinterest.com/HarlequinBooks